"You know, Ms. Hol
with her back to her porcl
bring you up in the bucket. Only accredited personnel are
supposed to go up." He paused. "Just like it's probably
against regulations for University instructors to get too
friendly with students in their class."

"It is," she said, feeling bold. "But if you can break
a rule, I can. Would you like to come in for a beer?"

"That may not be so wise. I'm an owner of this tree
business and owner of the bucket truck. I wasn't worried
about breaking that rule tonight. I knew it was safe for
you when I brought you up in the bucket. That's not the
way it is with you and the University. And you don't
know—" He hesitated.

"Know what?"

He smiled a little, as if joking. "Whether you'd be
safe alone in your house with me."

Praise for Patricia McAlexander

THE STUDENT IN CLASSROOM 6

"…With a killer on the loose and her job on the line, Katherine Holiday knows better than to act on her feelings for the sexy, intelligent student in the back of her college classroom. But the attraction is too strong to ignore. *The Student in Classroom Six* is a fast-paced romance with a dangerous edge that is easy to read and hard to put down…"

Lori Duffy Foster, author, Lisa Jamison Mystery Series

~*~

"…Smart characters, steamy romance and a dash of danger: the perfect recipe for a saucy, suspenseful read!"

Jon Jefferson, author of Wave of Terror

~*~

SHADOWS OF DOUBT (2021)

"A coming-of-age novel involving the dark underworld of college drug dealing…At once chilling and literary."

Molly Hurley Moran, author of Finding Susan

~*~

STRANGER IN THE STORM (2020)

"…A wonderful romance thriller…filled with twists, turns, and suspense…"

Still Moments Magazine

~*~

"…A page-turner…It could become a movie."

Jerome Loving, author of Jack and Norman

The Student in Classroom 6

by

Patricia McAlexander

This is a work of fiction. Names, characters, places, and incidents are either the product of the author's imagination or are used fictitiously, and any resemblance to actual persons living or dead, business establishments, events, or locales, is entirely coincidental.

The Student in Classroom 6

COPYRIGHT © 2022 by Patricia Jewell McAlexander

Cover Art by *Rae Monet, Inc.*

The Wild Rose Press, Inc.
PO Box 708
Adams Basin, NY 14410-0708
Visit us at www.thewildrosepress.com

Publishing History
First Edition, 2022
Trade Paperback ISBN 978-1-5092-4175-0
Digital ISBN 978-1-5092-4176-7

Published in the United States of America

Dedication

To my father, Albert Edward Jewell, who gave me my first typewriter, and my mother, Irene Fitch Jewell, who passed on to me her love of language

Prologue

Athens, Georgia, Monday, January 5, 2009

Dr. William Flatt, head of the English Department at the University of Georgia, looked out over the instructors and teaching assistants who had gathered for the last-minute meeting he'd called the day before the spring semester classes were to begin. About thirty men and women of various ages sat before him at student desks in the classroom, some with notebooks open. Others merely stared at him as they sipped from Styrofoam coffee cups. As usual, he held separate meetings for this group and the regular English faculty made up of tenured and tenure-track professors.

"Most of you know why I've called this meeting," he began. "It has to do with the unfortunate event that occurred on campus outside Psychology Hall on the last day of fall semester exams."

The newspapers had thoroughly covered the murder of Dr. Amanda Morang, a popular young assistant professor of psychology, whose body was found in the bushes in the early morning near her building's exterior glass-windowed elevator. Someone could have been outside the night before, watching her in it as it descended. There were signs of a struggle: branches had been broken, her clothes were torn, her purse lay open beside her, its contents strewn—though her wallet and

1

cell phone were still there. She had been shot with three nine-millimeter bullets: one in her arm, another in her leg, a third—the fatal one—in her heart.

The police investigated a large number of potential suspects: her ex-husband, her many students and colleagues, men she'd dated since her divorce, the clients she and her graduate students had been seeing in the university's Psychology Clinic. So far, their efforts led to nothing. People began to speculate that the killer may have been someone she didn't know at all, a lurker on the campus who saw her leaving the building late that night. She often, especially since her divorce, worked in her office long after everyone else had left.

Dr. Flatt picked up his notes uncomfortably. "We must learn from what happened. The university has increased campus security, especially during the evening hours. And I called you here to remind you all again—both men and women—of departmental policy: do not be alone in your office with a student unless the door is open; do not socialize off campus with your current students, do not work in your office in the evenings or on weekends without first ensuring the building's outside door's locked; and, if possible, avoid working on campus at night while alone…That about covers it, I think. But overall, just be aware and use common sense. Are there any questions?"

One of the men asked, "Have the police uncovered any new leads in the murder?"

"If they have, they're not making them public."

A young teaching assistant raised her hand. "Is this the first murder ever on campus?"

"There was one other—and that was back in 1918, a murder-suicide. Some students let a friend just back from service in France use their dorm room to meet with his girlfriend. He shot her, then shot himself. Nothing on campus since then." He paused. "Anything else?" No one spoke. "All right. So when classes start tomorrow, remember our policies and be careful. The police still think the murderer might be someone who works or studies here on campus. If any of you have information that might help in the investigation, be sure to call the Athens police department's hotline number. Meeting adjourned."

Katherine Holiday, one of the young new instructors who had completed her master's degree at the university just the year before, put her note pad back in her purse and stood. Out in the hall her officemate, Linda Wilson, joined her. "I have a friend in the Psychology Department. He says Dr. Morang was attractive and, since her divorce, not always as professional as she should have been. She sometimes went out with her graduate students and traveled with them to conferences."

"He's blaming the victim," said Katherine.

"Okay, you're right. But we're young too, and let's face it, not bad looking. It's scary to think there might be some kind of predator out there."

The two walked to the elevator and Katherine punched *B* for basement, where their office, like many of the offices of the instructors and teaching assistants, was located. "I don't think we need to panic. As Dr. Flatt said, we should use our common sense."

Though her awareness of potential danger on campus was heightened, Katherine really did not feel afraid. She never worked alone on campus late at night, and she always tried to be professional with her teaching.

She put her long honey-colored hair up in a bun for class and wore conservative clothes—pants suits, blazers. None of her students had ever seemed threatening. In her day classes last semester, the first- and second-year students were good kids, if sometimes immature, and the adults in her Tuesday-Thursday evening class had been eager to learn. Besides, she thought, most murders she saw on television or read about in the news took place in cities like New York or Atlanta, or in backwoods areas as in the movie *Deliverance*. They were far less likely to happen on college campuses, and until this one, definitely not at today's University of Georgia.

Chapter One

His orange T-shirt was sweaty under his jacket, and he still felt grains of sawdust against his skin. He'd been up in the bucket all day, taking down a diseased tree. He wouldn't have time to shower and change before class, but that didn't matter. As his teammates finished blowing off the twigs and leaves from the area and putting the machinery away in the transport truck, Tyler McHenry climbed into his own pickup. He turned the key in the ignition, then peeled off from the worksite, on his way to the Continuing Education Center to take English 101, the course that used to be called freshman composition.

Freshman composition—and he was twenty-six years old! All this for his mother. Well, she probably deserved it, after all the years she had home schooled him, filling his head with the classics, art, languages. When he'd switched to the public high school in his junior year, he was way ahead of everyone else. What he'd needed to catch up on then was social life, team sports, girls. And he had.

Stopped at a red light, Tyler downshifted and flipped on the truck radio. Country music filled the cab. His two public high school years had been fun, but he hadn't wanted to do what so many other kids did after graduation—go on to college. It somehow seemed frivolous. He was happy to work for his father's tree service—as he had already been, part-time, for most of his life. Being outdoors, high up in the trees, the cables around his waist…the teamwork with his father and his crew, making some money…that was what he wanted.

His mother, of course, disapproved. She thought a college degree was essential for him, for anyone. But his father had done well and never went beyond high school. He had taken over the family business just as Tyler himself would do someday. Already he was not only a partner in the McHenry Tree Service, but co-owner.

"What about all I taught you?" his mother demanded. "And your top scores on the SAT?"

"I'm keeping all you gave me—up here," Tyler had told her, tapping his head.

He didn't tell her about the novel he was writing, though. It would excite her too much, make her even more adamant that he go to college. But when she was diagnosed with pancreatic cancer that late fall of 2008, and they learned she had only a short time to live, he reconsidered. It would make her last days so happy to think he was going to college after all. Just under the deadline he signed up for a spring semester course at the Continuing Education Center that, as he told his mother, could be applied toward a degree. And the harried advisor, paying little attention to his background, placed him in one of the few remaining evening class openings left—this introductory English course.

Tyler shrugged and signed the form. The class didn't matter. He didn't plan to continue for a degree anyway—he'd just let his mother think he would. A writing course might actually be a kind of diversion and, being a first-year course, certainly easy for him. He didn't want to have to spend a lot of time studying when he was already working more than full-time.

In his work clothes, he would probably look different from the other students. He was almost glad. He *was* different. He drew up to the Center parking lot and found a space. This college class might be rather interesting to observe, if not fully participate in.

****

At the Continuing Education Center, about to enter the first meeting of her adult evening composition class of the semester, Katherine checked herself in the restroom mirror with critical gray-green eyes. Her day classes, one sophomore literature and two first-year composition. were scheduled on Mondays, Wednesdays, and Fridays in Park Hall on the main campus. Her first time to meet with them would be the next day.

Tonight's evening class, held in the University's more accessible Continuing Education Center a few blocks away, would meet on Tuesdays and Thursdays from six-thirty to eight-fifteen with a break about midway through—so it came out to the equivalent of the three-times-a-week day classes. The break time gave the night students a chance to confer individually and in person with their teacher, for often they could not stay after class.

This evening she was, after Dr. Flatt's meeting, more intent than usual on making a proper impression. She had always been aware that the persona she projected was especially important for these older, "non-traditional" students. She was younger than most of them. Yes, her clothes tonight looked appropriately professional—a charcoal-gray blazer, high-necked white blouse, black slacks. She tucked straying strands of hair tightly into her bun, freshened her natural-colored lip gloss, and picked up her briefcase. She was ready.

Taking a deep breath, she walked down the corridor and entered the assigned classroom—number six. Students were filing in, taking seats in the armed desk chairs, chatting, checking their phones. She placed her briefcase on the table beside the lectern and arranged her handouts in neat piles. The clock on the back wall clicked to 6:30.

"It's time to begin," she said, projecting her voice authoritatively. "Put away your phones. I am Ms. Holiday, and this is English 101, section 4E."

As she spoke, Katherine looked out over the faces before her. A few of the students were about her age—in their twenties; others probably ranged from thirty to fifty. These all no doubt had day jobs. Then there were the retirees who had time to come back now for a college degree—a plump woman with graying hair, a bald man with golfer's tan, a small, humpbacked, shaky little man who looked like a white-haired pixie.

The younger women were dressed in office attire—stockings, heels—and had manicured, polished nails. They were probably secretaries or, as the retail stores now called them, sales associates. The black woman had love knots in her hair and a colorful pleated skirt. A few of the men had on jackets and ties; the others, including the three black men in the class, wore neat sports shirts and slacks. Salesmen, perhaps.

A tan young man with sun-streaked hair and blue eyes, maybe in his late twenties, lounged in a row by himself over on the far-left side. He was probably some kind of laborer—he had on worn jeans, heavy work shoes, and a plain orange T-shirt that revealed broad shoulders and muscular arms. The other students looked at her with serious expectation. He looked at her with a kind of detached amusement. These were all familiar, safe student types, except for that non-academic-looking young man.

She proceeded to call the roll from the printout the administration had sent her. There was usually a student, maybe two, who were in the wrong class. Students responded with a "here" or raised their hand as she said their name, sometimes correcting her pronunciation. "James Waffle," she read.

"Wa-*fell*," he said.

She made a note of it. Once class began, she, like most teachers, would call students by their first names, informally. Her father, an English professor retired from Colgate University in upstate New York, had always called the men Mr., the women Mrs. or Miss—or in later years, Ms.

"Is there anyone whose name I did not call?" she asked when she reached the end of the list.

The muscular young man raised his hand. "Tyler McHenry." He stood and handed her a slip of paper. It was a late registration form.

She took the form, perused it, and added his name to her list. "Anyone else?"

Everyone was quiet. No lost students, this time. "Here is the class description," she said, picking up the first stack of papers. "I'll go over it with you now." She handed out a little pile of handouts to the first student in every row, who passed them back to those behind, except for Tyler McHenry, in that row by himself.

The first heading was "Course Goal."

"Our general goal is to improve your writing. Our specific goal is to prepare you for success in your future college courses, which often require writing," she said. "It has been a while since most of you were in high school, so practice with writing should be helpful." The second heading was "Textbook." She described the required book of essays, short fiction, and grammar lessons that she had selected for the class, now available at the campus bookstore. She thought the readings in it would interest the students and provide good topics for their essays.

Last was the heading "Course Description and Grading Policies." First she described the Essay Portfolio: "Over the semester you will write and revise seven essays of two to three typed double-spaced pages. Topics will be based on the assigned readings. I will read and comment on each of your essays and assign a grade. If you wish, you can revise based on my comments for another grade. You will keep all your printed-out, graded essays in a folder. At the end of the semester you will hand your folder in to me; I'll review it in a conference with you. Your essays will count for eighty percent of your grade, and the final exam, a take-home essay, will count the remaining twenty."

Then came the part that, with these adults, she was a little embarrassed about. Perhaps she should have made this section different for her evening class; after all, adults were usually more disciplined and motivated as students. But, as with her day classes, she told them that their physical *and* mental presence in class was very important, that they were allowed only four absences unless they had documentation regarding illness. And three tardies, she said, would equal one absence. After that number of absences, she would subtract half a point from their average for each class missed. She used the policy mainly to guarantee regular attendance with her often party-loving young day students. It worked.

She acknowledged Tyler McHenry's raised hand. "Will you, Ms. Holiday, ever be late or absent?"

His tone was not insolent. He had a soft, Southern voice, and he spoke with a kind of lazy, teasing smile. It was the question itself that she considered insolent. A dark-haired student at the back of the room with a sharp nose and beady eyes—one of the salesmen in jacket and tie—briefly snickered.

She regarded Tyler straight on. "I will never be late or absent." She swept her eyes over the other students, making eye contact, especially with that dark-haired student. "Any other questions?"

There were none. The dark-haired student sobered. The room was quiet.

"Then," she said, "here is the syllabus for the first three weeks. As you see, your first essay will be due on our next class. The topics will not grow out of our reading, but will be based on personal experience. For this assignment, we will focus on the elements of the essay and begin work on correct grammar and mechanics. We will also discuss the importance of specific details and examples to prove your points."

She handed out the syllabus which included the topic for the first essay: *Write a 500-750 word essay describing one to three characteristics of a teacher, relative, or fellow employee. Tell little stories or anecdotes to illustrate.*

"I will share, anonymously, some of the best essays in class, and we will discuss why they are effective," she told them. "And perhaps some of you will have suggestions as to how they could be made even more effective. If any of you would object to my using your essay, please write a note to that effect on it when you hand it in." She hoped these topics would not only be fun for the students, but also help break the ice in the class. Seldom did anyone request that their essays not be used for discussion.

She looked at the clock on the wall opposite her. "It's seven-fifteen. Let's take a ten-minute break and, when you come back, we'll discuss the elements of the essay and define some basic terms of grammar."

The students began to chat and stretch, and some walked out of the classroom to the rest rooms. Katherine glanced over her plans for the next hour. She would show a chart defining the basic elements of the essay on an overhead projector—introduction with thesis statement, body paragraphs with topic sentences and evidence, conclusion. Then she would move to parts of speech, which they would need to review for upcoming lessons on grammar. Adult students, especially the older ones, usually liked the lessons on grammar.

"Ahem." As someone approached the lectern, Katherine looked up. A gray-haired woman with bright red lipstick handed her a sheet of paper. Her name, Katherine remembered, was Carrie Greene.

"Ms. Holiday, I write poetry. I was wondering if you would look at a couple of my poems."

Inwardly Katherine winced. Student poetry was often bad, and she did not like to hurt any writer's feelings. Poetry was so intimate. Aloud she said, "Of course," extending her hand and taking the sheet. "Some of what we discuss in here will relate to poetry. The use of concrete details and images, for example."

"Concrete?" asked the woman.

"I mean by that, specific details—appeals to the senses…Well, you'll see." Katherine smiled.

"I know I'll just love this class," the woman gushed.

Katherine raised her eyes beyond the woman and saw the student Tyler, still lounging in his seat, looking at her. His eyes were very blue in his tan face and again, there was that look of amusement on his face. He seemed to know her feelings about the woman and her poetry. Katherine looked quickly away.

****

At eight-fifteen Katherine stood on the curb outside the Continuing Education Center, waiting to cross the street to the parking area where she'd left her car. Night had come on, and students were streaming out of the building to go to their own cars. She felt a combination of fatigue and exhilaration. Overall, her class had gone well, but it had taken a lot of energy not just to prepare, but to put on the classroom performance, to win the students' respect and to get them to share her enthusiasm for writing.

The light turned to "Walk." She crossed quickly to the parking lot, pulled her keys from her purse and, when she had reached the appropriate distance in the parking lot row, clicked. Her car lights flashed a welcoming response.

A truck was coming fast along the row, heading toward the exit. Some kind of lively guitar music was issuing from its speakers. On the truck door was painted "McHenry Tree Service." She remembered the name on the late registration slip: *McHenry, Tyler.* Apparently, he was an arborist. She looked up to the open driver's side window and there he was, thick hair ruffled by the wind, elbow resting on the window ledge. Their eyes met. He

13

raised his hand in a kind of salute, and a slight smile deepened the dimples on each side of his mouth like parentheses.

****

The first assignment was easy, Tyler thought, and the teacher was pretty. She seemed too young to be teaching a college course. He should not have asked her whether she herself would ever be tardy or absent—she hadn't liked that. And he hadn't meant to make that weird guy in the back of the room laugh. He'd just wanted her to relax, loosen up a little.

Late on Wednesday evening, Tyler dumped his pizza carton in the recycling bin and went over to the couch in his doublewide, situated far behind his parents' rambling nineteenth-century farm house. His laptop was on the coffee table before him, where he kept it for his writing, often done into the early morning hours. This assignment wouldn't take long. He thought he would describe his mother.

He stared at the screen for a few minutes. What could he say, with all his mixed feelings for her—resentment, rebellion, love? Memories floated up in his mind like the "answer" slips in the black gypsy globe he remembered playing with as a child.

He was twelve years old and reading the Iliad *as he ate his lunch sandwich. His mother would discuss the work with him in a few minutes. He could picture the battles, the characters, the ships, even had an image in his mind of the beautiful Helen. His mother came to the door of his room, where she had sent him with the book an hour earlier. "It's time," she said.*

He got up and followed her downstairs to her study, a sunny room with plants and a view of her flowers on the patio. *"I want you to write a short essay first,"* she told him. *"I want you to answer the question: Was Ulysses unethical in using the Trojan horse to gain access to the city of Troy? I'll give you twenty minutes."*

Interesting question. Tyler nibbled at the top of his ballpoint pen. He knew she wanted not just an answer to her question, but correct grammar, good organization. So he had to think a little first. Perhaps employing the horse was unethical, a lie. But the war needed to be over, and after ten years it seemed to be the only way. Did the end justify the means? Maybe overall it was war that was the evil, not the lie.

He began to write. A knock came on the door of the study. His mother expelled an angry breath and moved quickly to the door. He heard his father's voice. "I want to take Tyler to our work site this afternoon. We have a big job—a seventy-five-foot pin oak to take down. It will be good for him to go."

"He's writing an essay," his mother hissed, meaning it to be a whisper.

"You've had him all morning. The boy needs to get outside."

Tyler stopped writing. "I can finish this tonight, Mom."

"You need to finish it now. You'll lose your train of thought."

"Come on, son," said his father, entering the room. *"You've done your study time for the day."*

"I'll remember my train of thought, Mom." Tyler put down his pen, stood, and preceded his father out of the room. He did not look at his mother, knowing the blaze of frustration that would be in her eyes.

His mother had groomed him for some kind of

brilliant academic career with her study sessions. He was so gifted, she said—he'd win a scholarship to an Ivy League school like Harvard or one of those West Coast universities—Stanford, Berkeley. She still hadn't stopped talking to him about earning a degree, although he was a man now, working full time, not even living at home exactly, but in the doublewide on the back lot, and now her hopes centered on the University of Georgia. When his father had taken his side after high school and made him partner in the family tree service, she resented that deeply. He saw how she looked at the two of them as they went off together in the morning to their work.

He decided to do a portrait of her in one of her bitter, sarcastic moods, the kind of mood he tried not to respond to, just avoid. His fingers began tapping, moving faster as he went.

****

The evening class students handed in their essays on Thursday, and over that weekend, Katherine read them. Even when their writing needed work, she enjoyed the anecdotes—Carrie Green's about her nephew who'd fought in Afghanistan, James Waffle's about his high school football coach, the dark-haired student's—his name was Gene Whittaker—about his supervisor in Howe's Home Supplies appliance department. She selected several of the better ones to share with the classes on overheads. They would discuss why these essays were effective. She felt giving positive examples was a good method of teaching; they would help those whose writing had been weaker.

But one essay disturbed her, and it was Tyler's, about his mother. It was head and shoulders above all the others. She wished she could use it as one of the models, but he had written "Do Not Share" at the top of the paper. She wouldn't have used it anyway, for surely it was not his—it was too effective, too professional sounding. That must be why he didn't want the class to see it. She was horrified to discover a case of plagiarism, though she could not find anything like his essay on the internet. Why hadn't she dealt with the plagiarism issue in her handout? She gave the essay no grade, but wrote merely, "See me after class."

On Tuesday evening many of the adults in the class enthusiastically discussed the essays projected on the screen, and she felt there were several learning moments. Tyler McHenry kept mostly silent, just observing. At the end of the first half of the class, she returned the students' essays. The second half was devoted to illustrating some of the more common grammar and mechanical errors she'd found in their papers. At eight-fifteen, the class was over and the students left, a few pausing on their way out to speak with her. Finally, only Tyler remained. She knew no other class was scheduled in her classroom now, so she could use it for meetings like this.

She felt a little nervous—this discussion might be difficult. She was glad to hear the chatter of students in the hall outside the classroom. Remembering Dr. Flatt's admonition, she left the door wide open and motioned Tyler forward. They sat in chairs across from each other at the table next to her lectern.

"I'd like to talk to you a little about your essay," she said. "Could I see it again?" He pulled it out of the spiral bound notebook he carried with him and handed it to her. She noted his hands. They were large and strong.

She unfolded his paper and ran her finger down the typed lines. "You use the word *sardonic* here," she said.

"Can you explain what you mean by that?"

He shrugged a shoulder slightly, shifted in his chair. "It means kind of mocking, I guess," he said. "Maybe sarcastic. It's hard to get an exact synonym. You didn't like that word?"

"No, the word is fine," she said. She looked back down at his essay and ran her finger further along the lines. "Here," she said, "You say that your mother has an *acerbic* wit. Can you tell me what that means?"

"I gave an example."

"But I'd like you to define that word."

He thought. "Sharp, stinging—like an arrow puncture or a wasp bite." He looked intent, earnest. There was no laughing mockery in his expression now. His voice had a pleasant warmth and softness to her Northerner's ears.

"That's a good definition," she said. She'd made a photocopy of his essay in case she wanted to pursue the plagiarism question, but she saw, with relief, that there was no need to. She handed back his paper. "I was able to develop a real sense of your mother from this. She sounds…interesting."

He stuck the paper into his notebook. "She would like you, I think."

Feeling her cheeks flush, Katherine rose. "Your writing is excellent. I didn't put a grade on your essay. I'll tell you what it is now—A plus."

He rose too and slung his jacket over his shoulder. "I'm glad you liked it. Good night, Ms. Holiday."

"Good night, Tyler."

But by the door he abruptly stopped as if a thought has struck him, then turned to her. "You thought this wasn't my work, didn't you?"

"Well, I—" Katherine began, but, not waiting for an answer, he turned back to the hall and strode off, an angry rigidity in his spine.

She stared at the empty doorway. It had gone so well—then suddenly turned bad. *He's figured it out. He's mad at me. Now he may want to drop my class. And he would be such an interesting student.* She gathered up her papers. *Do I owe him an apology? No, I don't. I have identified plagiarism cases this way before, when the student had no idea of the meaning of words he had used in his essay. What I did by questioning him was prove he really wrote that paper.*

****

Out on the Atlanta Highway, Tyler knew he was driving too fast, but he didn't care.

Shit, I don't have to put up with this. My mother has been difficult enough. I don't have to put up with some girl-teacher questioning me, judging me, not even believing I wrote my essay. He pulled in at the Dark Owl Lounge. He could use a beer and some social life. As he entered, a group of young women called to him and waved. He went over to them.

"Where have you been? I haven't seen you in forever," said Tonya, she with the long dark hair and the curvy body he knew quite well.

"Yeah, too long," said Tyler, putting his hand on the back of her neck. Music started from the country band up on the little stage. "Come on." He led her out into the floor for a dance, waving at the waitress and pointing at the table. "A Bud."

"I thought you'd forgotten me," Tonya said.

"I wouldn't do that." He twirled her around, feeling his anger die down.

"I've been here a lot of nights. Where have you been?"

He shook his head, "Guess I should have been here." They went back to the table where his bottle of beer waited. He took it, tipped his head back, and drank.

"Want to come back to my place? I have a lot more of that." She indicated the bottle.

"A tempting offer. Tonya the Temptress." He laughed and finished off the bottle.

"Well, then?"

He shook his head and put the bottle back on the table. "Can't. Another time." He saw her begin to pout. "Soon," he said, and gave her a quick kiss on the mouth, pulling back as she moved closer to him. "Bye, babe."

"Bye, Tyler," the other girls at the table chorused.

He turned, went out the door, climbed into his truck. He felt a little better now.

Well, shit, she liked my essay. She said the grade was A plus.

****

Katherine felt pinpricks of conscience over the next five days. Tyler McHenry's essay on his mother had characterized the woman as vividly as if part of a novel. If the description had not been published, it should be. *Perhaps I was biased by his workman appearance.* Although she continued to justify her questioning of Tyler McHenry over the next two days, she was bothered by the anger he'd shown as he walked away and wondered, if he came back on Thursday evening, how he would act in class.

She looked up McHenry's Tree Service on the internet. The business was co-owned by Tyler and his father. The photos showed a large bucket truck, Tyler up in a bucket, cutting limbs off a tree with a chain saw, Tyler standing on a huge hollow tree stump. In that photo, he looked like a warrior over a defeated prey—but she knew the tree had been felled not in battle or for the thrill of sport, but out of some kind of necessity.

He must want to start work on a college degree, she thought—but why? He would surely take over his father's business someday. He would not need a college degree for that. And he already wrote so well! And what was he doing in her class anyway? He should have placed out of it—he should have been in an honors class.

The following Tuesday evening when she entered the classroom, Tyler was not there. She spoke to individual students and returned Carrie's poems, saying as encouraging words as she could. The wall clock hands moved to six-thirty. Tyler's seat remained empty. Outwardly she kept her smile, her enthusiasm as they discussed the assigned reading in her packet of photocopied material—Dick Gregory's autobiographical "Shame," about a little boy whose teacher disliked him—and the worrisome thoughts renewed. Had he dropped the course?

At seven-fifteen, they stopped for the break. Carrie came up to her and said, "Thank you again for reading my poems. I have two more here for you."

I will have to stop this. "Thank you, but I'd better focus on your essay writing during this semester. I think this class will help you improve your poems."

"Oh, I should have known you'd be too busy reading everyone's essays to critique my poems," Carrie said. "I am so sorry! Maybe after this semester ends."

"Maybe," said Katherine with a smile. "But you might consider taking a creative writing class as an elective." She turned to go out to the rest room. Hurrying into the hall, she found Tyler leaning against the wall by the classroom door. She drew in a surprised breath.

He turned his head and looked down at her, with his little smile. "Well, this is tardy number one."

He was quite tall—Katherine, fairly tall herself, felt small beside him. His chambray shirt had dark moisture stains under the arms, now dried in the warmth of the building. A few flecks of sawdust—light wood bits—were in his hair. She could smell the fresh-cut wood.

"How long have you been out here? You should not have waited to come in."

"I didn't want to disrupt the class."

"You were working late."

He gave a brief affirmative nod.

"We discussed the assigned reading. I missed you. I know you would have had interesting things to say about it." She had not wanted to apologize directly for questioning his essay. She hoped this statement would suffice.

The corners of his eyes crinkled a little. "I'm sure you did fine."

He pushed away from the wall and walked into the classroom. It seemed that he'd accepted her indirect apology. She looked after him for a moment. In the restroom, she examined her reflection in the mirror. Tendrils of her hair had loosened from her bun, and her cheeks again were flushed. Annoyed that she had not kept up her teacher image more effectively, she splashed her face with water and neatened her bun. She would be giving a lesson on grammar when she returned.

Chapter Two

Throughout February, Tyler got into the rhythm of attending the composition class on Tuesday and Thursday evenings. He even found himself looking forward to it. The essays and stories assigned were interesting, and to his surprise it was fun to be part of the class discussions. Writing had been a lonely pastime. Now he had an appreciative audience for his work—sometimes just Ms. Holiday and sometimes, when she shared his later papers, the whole class.

He liked the students he'd come to know, but most of all, he had to admit, he enjoyed watching the teacher up there at the front of the room. She was so cute with her enthusiasm about writing, with her hair sometimes coming loose, her eyes sparkling with excitement. And she was smart, he had to admit—in some ways like the best side of his mother when she had homeschooled him. He thought this Ms. Holiday had come to respect him and his work, to want his opinion in class. He liked getting her comments on his papers, always positive, though sometimes with—he had to admit it—good questions and suggestions.

He began to wonder about her life outside of the classroom. She wore no ring. Was she dating someone? What did she do for fun? But he should not think about any of that. He would never see her outside the four walls of Classroom Six unless it was glimpses of her going to her car in the Center parking lot.

Nevertheless, he did not go back to the Dark Owl Lounge where Tonya and her friends hung out. Instead, when he had the time, he began working on his novel with renewed intent.

****

As the weeks passed, thoughts of the still unsolved campus murder mostly faded from Katherine's mind. She kept busy planning her classes and reading the stacks of student essays. When grading the evening class papers, she always saved Tyler's work for last; it was her reward. She liked to imagine that he was writing personally to her, although in her responding comments, she tried to remain the detached, though friendly, English teacher: "Interesting point. Could you expand on this idea?"…"Unclear pronoun reference"… "Convincing argument, but what about…?"

As she read his essays with rapt attention, she mentally pictured him. She liked his tawny hair, his dimples, and that full lower lip. She liked his muscular build, the way his biceps were revealed when he leaned back in his chair and put his arms behind his head. During the breaks, when he went out into the hall, she liked the way he moved—with a kind of unconscious, sinewy grace.

And Katherine realized she felt something for this Tyler McHenry that she'd never before felt for a student. She was *physically attracted* to him. Some of the girls in the class were obviously aware of him this way as well. They'd approach him to talk during the breaks, laughing as they looked up at him, tossing back their hair.

As she made her green-inked notations on her papers, she wondered: Did he ever wish to talk with her, as he did with those girls—and not limit their exchanges to classroom discussions or notes on his essays? There often seemed to be a warm glow in his eyes as he watched her there at the lectern. If they were not a teacher and student, but just themselves at a singles bar, would he come over to her, start a conversation, maybe offer to buy her a drink?

If he did, I would accept.

What crazy fantasies to have, she sometimes thought, and she reminded herself of the murder on campus and departmental policies regarding faculty and students. Was she daydreaming this way because she hadn't dated anyone for almost a year? She had not been involved with a man since her fellow grad student Robert Mason, who'd earned his Ph.D. the previous June and accepted a job as an assistant professor at Texas A&M. He'd suggested she move to Texas with him, but there would have been no job there for her, and the University of Georgia had offered her a three-year instructorship. She realized her feelings for Robert were not enough to make the leap of abandoning her friends in Georgia and her college teaching career. And so when he left, she stayed in Athens; it was a natural, amicable end to their relationship.

Henry Armstid, a young lawyer who lived down the street from the Fosters' home where she was house-sitting for the year, had approached her a few times during the fall. But although he was nice, she just couldn't relate to him romantically. She told herself, her officemate, and her women friends she didn't have time for a new relationship right now.

****

After that first essay, her topics did not ask students

to write about their personal experiences. They called for analytical discussions of techniques or ideas in the readings. So she learned nothing more of Tyler's background until one early March Thursday when they discussed a story they were to write about over the weekend—Ernest Hemingway's "Indian Camp."

The story, about a doctor-father who takes his young son with him to attend a difficult childbirth in an Indian (Native American) camp, had always generated good discussion and interesting essays. Katherine had selected it thinking the undergraduates would especially like it, since she saw it as an initiation story. In it, a young boy witnesses and reacts to the horrors of the difficult childbirth—a Caesarian—and the woman's husband who, trapped in the bunk above her with a foot injury, can no longer stand witnessing her pain and commits suicide. The older students in the evening classes, however, always responded to the story equally well. This evening was no exception, though now the students became very involved in discussing, not the character of the boy, but the character of his father, the doctor.

"That doctor is a complete male chauvinist!" said Maureen strongly. She was one of the sales associates in the class. "He doesn't care about the woman's pain. He says her screams are 'not important.' "

"All he wanted to do is show off to his son," put in Betty, a petite blonde who sat in the row next to Tyler's, her desk across the aisle from his. "The doctor should never have taken him when he went to help the Indian woman. He even makes that poor child hold the afterbirth basin."

Gene Whittaker, the dark-haired young man sitting at the back of the room who'd laughed when Tyler asked

Katherine if she'd ever be late, now turned his eyes on her and raised his hand. What was *he* going to say?

He'd made her slightly uneasy as the semester advanced. She thought his black eyes looked a little strange—one of them turned slightly inward—and he always watched her so fixedly that, along with his sharp nose, he reminded her of a bird of prey. Though his vocabulary was good and he inserted sometimes unique poetic images into his essays, his writing was disorganized, often veering off on tangents. And his comments in class discussion missed the mark somehow—they were off the wall and sometimes even a bit off color. Tonight, he was true to form. "Maybe," he said, with a little smirk, "Nick's father just wanted to give the kid some sex education."

Before Katherine could respond, Betty turned around in her seat to regard Gene angrily. "It had nothing to do with *sex*. He calls his son an intern. He's like so many fathers who selfishly want their sons to be just like them, without regard for the sons' feelings. In this case, it's almost like child abuse."

As the class murmured agreement, Tyler's voice was heard over the rest then, his southern accented voice strong with conviction. "There is nothing wrong with a father teaching his son about his profession," he said. "The doctor is a good teacher—he explains childbirth in terms the boy can understand. He couldn't know this birth would have such a bad outcome. And he obviously *is* skilled and experienced, performing major surgery in primitive circumstances—using a jack knife for the incision and sewing it up with gut leaders."

The class silenced. All looked at Tyler.

"But he doesn't care about the woman's pain," said

Betty after a moment.

"It's not that he doesn't care about the pain. He can't do anything about it. He doesn't have any anesthetic. A surgeon can't do his job well if he doesn't have scientific detachment from his patients." Tyler glanced at Katherine. "His or her patients." He looked back at the class. "That's why some doctors won't operate on family members or relatives."

"What is Hemingway trying to show by the suicide of the woman's husband?" asked Katherine. She spoke generally to the class, but she wanted to know what Tyler would say.

Carrie spoke up first. "He's showing that pain and suffering *are* important—they do have consequences," she said. "The doctor should have known that."

Tyler spoke. "The doctor was focusing on the patient. As soon as he could, he checked on the husband. And as soon as he saw what the husband had done, he said, 'Take Nick out of the shanty.' "

Now he looked mainly at Katherine. "I don't think we can say the doctor is a tragic hero like Oedipus, but there are parallels. When he sees the husband has committed suicide, he feels horrible guilt— like Oedipus did when he found out he'd married his mother. And what happened, in both cases was not their fault. Oedipus didn't know the woman he married was his mother. The doctor didn't know the husband would commit suicide. And he doesn't take self-punishment as far as Oedipus, but he is obviously pretty devastated. His exhilaration is gone. He apologizes to Nick. He says he's sorry he brought him along, that it was an awful mess to put him through. And he tries his best to explain to Nick, as honestly but as gently as he can, what happened."

"Who is Oedipus?" Betty, sitting next to Tyler, whispered to him.

But Katherine asked him a question at the same time: "So you think the father, not Nick, is the focus of this story?"

Tyler glanced at Betty and then looked back to Katherine. "Hemingway may not have meant it to be, but yes," he said. "It's the father who changes and grows. Nick does not. He's still the little boy protected by his father. He has seen this horrible death, but at the end of the story he thinks he himself will never die."

The class was still. The clock on the wall clicked off a minute.

Katherine drew a deep breath and took her eyes from Tyler's. "You have all made some excellent comments," she said. "You'll have lots to think about when you write essays about this story. As you see, there is room for different points of view. The important thing is to give evidence for your arguments—especially by using facts and quotations from the story. I'll give out the topics in the next hour—oh, and I'll tell you the story of Oedipus, in case some of you don't know it." She paused. "Right now, it's time for a break."

She finished speaking to the students who came up to her with comments and questions. Then, as the students milled about or went out into the hall, she approached Tyler, who had just come back in and was at his seat. "You are the first student to make such a strong case for Nick's father."

"Maybe it's because he reminds me of my father," Tyler said. "He started taking me to work sites with him when I was very young. I did sometimes see accidents, kind of like that childbirth." He paused. "In my case, though, I *wanted* to follow in my father's profession."

****

That was how Katherine at last found out something more about Tyler's personal life. But she had no more chances to talk individually with him. As the weeks went by, she could only continue to be surprised and impressed by his intelligence, his writing ability, his class comments. But she knew she should put any romantic thoughts of Tyler out of her mind.

One Tuesday evening after her two hours of teaching, Katherine arrived home just as her phone buzzed. She pulled it from her purse and glanced at the screen. It was her friend Christy Ellis. Katherine threw her briefcase on the couch and slid the answer slider. "Hi, Christy."

"Hi, Katherine. I'm having a little dinner here Saturday, at six o'clock. Can you come?"

She'd known Christy in New York State; it was Christy who'd had relatives in Georgia and convinced Katherine to apply to UGA. She and Christy had roomed together here, along with Marian Wilson, another English grad student; they'd all received their master's degrees in English at the same time. While Katherine took the instructorship in the English Department with thoughts of later going on there for a PhD, Christy had married her long-term Athens boyfriend and taken a job as an English teacher at Athens Day Academy, a private school outside of Athens. Marian had taken a job with the local newspaper, the *Athens Banner*.

"Dinner sounds great," Katherine said. "Can I bring anything?"

"No, just yourself. I've also invited a UGA English professor who gave a guest lecture to my class last week,

Spenser Johns. He's new to the department this year. He's been hired here in part as a liaison to the UGA program at Oxford."

I guess Christy realizes I'm due for a relationship. Katherine tried to remember Spenser Johns. Instructors didn't attend faculty meetings, her office was in the basement of Park Hall, and she didn't remember seeing anyone new as she went to and from her classes. But his name sounded familiar. He must have been written up in the English department newsletter.

"I haven't met him," she said. *Yes, an English professor like that would be more appropriate for me.* And suddenly an episode from her high school life replayed in her mind, like a film. She had just seated herself at the dinner table with her parents on an April evening in 2002, eager to tell them her news....

"Guess what, Mom and Dad," she burst out. "Tony Brunetto has asked me to the junior prom."

Her father paused in reaching for his fork. "Ah, your high school's football star."

"I'd thought you'd be going with Jim Napler," said her mother.

"Jim and I are just friends." She and Jim were co-editors of the school newspaper, the Hamilton Central Bugle. Actually, she too had thought she'd be going to the prom with Jim, but she had danced with Tony a few times at the dances after the football games in the fall, and then, this spring, he'd suddenly begun talking to her in the halls and sitting with her at Sarris's ice cream parlor after the basketball games. And just that day he'd given her a ride home after school and asked her to be his date at the May junior prom. He was tall and ruggedly handsome for a high school boy, and she was

surprised and, yes, thrilled.

"I'd feel better if you were going with Jim," said her father. "He's a great kid, smart. I like him. Tony, as far as I can see, is pretty much just your typical high school jock."

She was horrified to hear the high school heart throb, the football and basketball star, who had thrilled her by choosing her to be his date, so coldly classified. "You are such an elitist, Dad!" she cried. "Sometimes I hate having a college professor as a father!" Pushing back her chair, she left the table and ran upstairs to her room. She threw herself on her bed, angry and tearful.

A few minutes later there was a knock on her door, and her mother entered. "Honey," she said. "Your father didn't mean anything by that. I think he's sorry. You seemed so happy when you told us you were going to the prom with Tony."

"Of course, I was happy. All the girls are crazy about Tony, and he asked me."

Her mother sat on the bed beside her and patted her back. "We'll have to go shopping for a dress for you."

"Dad's spoiled it all."

"Of course, he hasn't. You know Dad, he just likes academic types—they are more like him, like his favorite students. He has to realize this is nothing serious, just a date for a dance. And he and I both want you to have a good time. Come on downstairs. He wants to apologize."

She'd gone downstairs, her father had apologized, and she'd had a good time at the prom. But after she and Tony dated a few more times that summer, she'd decided her father was right. She and Tony didn't really have much in common.

****

Saturday at a little after six, Katherine rang Christy and Tom's doorbell, a bouquet of flowers from the garden behind the house where she was staying and a bottle of Merlot in her hands. Under her coat she wore a rose-colored cardigan over a long-sleeved scoop necked white jersey, a silk neck scarf, and pencil slim black slacks. Christy, tall and blonde in a long skirt and turtleneck sweater, answered the door. "Oh, what beautiful flowers. Come in."

She drew Katherine inside, took the wine and flowers, and led her to the living room, where her husband Tom sat on the couch beside a slim young man. "Katherine, this is Spenser Johns," Christy said. "Spenser, Katherine Holiday."

Spenser rose. His hair was brown and curly, and he wore gray slacks and a navy blazer. His skin was pale, his eyes a watery blue. "Pleased to meet you," he said, in a British accent. He held out a smooth white hand with long tapering fingers. She took it briefly. It felt cool and a bit moist.

"Hi, Katherine," Tom said, standing and giving her a hug.

As he took her coat, Christy turned toward the kitchen. "I'll just put these flowers in some water. And what would you like to drink, Katherine? We have some Riesling open, or would you prefer this Merlot?"

"The Riesling sounds fine," said Katherine.

"Tom, would you come and help me?"

Christy and her husband walked out, leaving Katherine there with Spenser Johns, who sat back down and crossed his legs. "So you're an instructor in the department, they tell me."

Katherine sat in an armchair facing him. "Yes, this

is my first year. When I finished my master's, they offered me a three-year contract to teach."

"You should have gone right on for a PhD," said Spenser. "Or were you not accepted into the program?"

"I didn't apply," said Katherine, slightly ruffled at the question. "I love teaching, and I wanted a break from taking classes and exams."

"You love teaching here? Amazing. After teaching at Oxford, I find the undergrads I teach here, overall, pretty vapid. And then this murder on campus. Poor Dr. Morang. I served on a faculty committee with her. She was a looker." He shook his head and took out a cigarette. "I hope you don't mind—this is an e-cigarette, no smoke, just water vapor."

"Oh, that's fine."

"It still gives you the nicotine effect—a nice little jolt." He smiled. "What field were you concentrating on for your MA?"

"American literature."

"You know what they say in England?" He blew out a puff of the water vapor smoke. "*Is* there any American literature?"

"I wonder if Christy needs any help," said Katherine, starting to get up.

"Sit down—Tom will give her all the help she needs. I'm in eighteenth-century British lit myself. I spent last summer in London doing research on Alexander Pope. I'm revising my dissertation into a book. Have you been to England?"

"As a child, with my parents," said Katherine. She looked up as Tom and Christy came back into the living room. Christy set a tray of crackers and cheese on the coffee table, and Tom handed Katherine a glass of wine.

Katherine took a long sip. *I need this*, she thought.

She indeed found wine a comfort as the evening went on. Over dinner, Spenser told them all about his research, his disdain for his current students, and his various publications. After they'd drunk after-dinner coffee in the living room and heard more of Spenser's exploits, Katherine said she had to go home. Christy came into the bedroom when Katherine was retrieving her coat. "I'm so sorry," Christy whispered. "Spenser was amusing when he taught a class to my high school honor students."

"Maybe he didn't think *they* were vapid," said Katherine.

Christy squeezed Katherine's arm sympathetically, and the two returned to the living room.

"Thank you so much, Christy and Tom," Katherine said. "Good night, Spenser. It was nice meeting you."

He took her hand. "Goodnight, Katherine. I guess I won't see you in that basement office, but when you're above ground for your classes, come by and see me."

"I'm sure you're too busy for company."

He smiled. "Not yours. So…Park Hall 220, about noon on a Monday, Wednesday, or Friday. I'll take you out for lunch."

She removed her hand from his. *I'm sorry, but that will never happen.*

At home, in her nightgown, she lay in bed, a pillow behind her head, and noted the stack of evening student papers on her dresser. She rose, rifled through them, found Tyler's, and began to read it. It was the perfect antidote to that horrible evening. His language, his wit, his insights. She laid his paper back down and closed her eyes. His hands were so different from Spenser Johns'—

they were strong and firm. His skin, not pasty white, but tan and smooth. His blue eyes, so bright and full of life.

The evening at Christy's hadn't eradicated her feelings for Tyler. It had made them stronger.

****

The following Monday morning, Katherine was leaving her eleven o'clock composition class. A figure who'd been standing in the hall stepped out to block her exit. "Hello, Ms. Holiday," said Spenser Johns.

Startled, she replied, "Oh, hello, Spenser."

"I thought we could go to lunch. The Broad Street Grill has a good chicken dish and strawberry praline pie."

Katherine tried to think of an excuse. "I'm sorry, I've packed a lunch and I've got papers to grade."

"I looked up your schedule. You're finished with your morning classes. You need a break."

She did not want to alienate a professor when she might apply to the PhD program in a couple of years. How could she avoid this invitation diplomatically? Some prevarication, perhaps. "Spenser, I should tell you—I'm dating someone steadily." *Actually, I'm thinking of someone steadily.*

"Your friend Christy told me you were free."

"I haven't told her about him yet. This relationship has just begun."

"And you weren't with him Saturday night?"

"He—he was out of town. So thank you, Spenser, for asking me to lunch, but I thought I should tell you about the situation."

His lips were pinched. "Even so, maybe you'd like a conversation with a real faculty member."

"Not today. And I consider myself a real faculty

member, too. Even if I am just an instructor."

"Of course." He smiled at her wryly. "But perhaps I can help if you apply to the doctoral program here."

"Thank you. Remember, though, I'm not in your field. I'd want to get a PhD in American literature. You know, the literature you say the Brits think doesn't exist."

Suddenly thinking of another, better excuse to give as to why she couldn't go to lunch, she looked at her watch. "I've got to get back to my office. A student is supposed to be coming by. Thanks again, Spenser."

She hurried down the hall, feeling his eyes at her back. She was not happy that she had lied about being in a relationship, at least not a real-life one. And yes, she had probably antagonized him. Some of her friends, like her officemate, might say that was not a smart thing to do. But that was because he might have some power in the department—not because he might be the campus murderer.

Chapter Three

On a Thursday evening in early April, with only about a month in the semester to go, Katherine was having supper in her house before leaving to teach her class. And as usual, she was running a little late. She finished her meal, threw her briefcase into the passenger seat of her car, and drove rapidly down the driveway, glad she lived so close to the campus.

But at the driveway's end, she slammed on the brakes. The shiny, leafy branches of a Southern Magnolia barricaded the road. At least a third of the huge tree across the street next to the sidewalk had split off, leaving a gash in the main trunk like a lightning strike, though there had been no storm. Katherine was a prisoner in her own driveway.

She got out of the car and joined the gathering neighbors. "It just fell," one said. "I heard the *whoosh*."

"Lucky no cars were parked on the street."

"Lucky no one was on the sidewalk when it came down," another said. "It could have killed someone."

"I've called the city. They'll be sending out crews to clear the road."

Katherine was frantic. "But I need to get to my class *now.*"

Henry Armstid, the young lawyer who lived down the street, moved toward her. "I'll take you," he said. "It isn't blocking my driveway."

She breathed a sigh of relief. "Oh, thank you, Henry." She retrieved her briefcase, which he gallantly took from her, and she walked with him to his driveway, dodging the branches that also filled the sidewalk. But she knew she surely would be late.

"Your class is in the Continuing Education Center?" asked Henry, once they were in his car, a shiny black Mercedes.

"Yes, you can drop me off at the back door, the one by the parking lot."

"You'll need a ride home too, won't you?"

"Yes—yes I will."

"I'll pick you up—what time shall I come?"

Because Henry had been trying to date Katherine for some time, this would be somewhat awkward, but she was grateful for his offer. "About a quarter until nine."

He drew up to the indicated door. "I'll pick you up here then."

"Thank you so much, Henry."

Clutching her briefcase, she got quickly out of the car. She rushed inside the building and down the hall to Classroom Six. When she pulled open the door, the clock at the back of the room said six-forty. The students, all in their seats, were surprisingly quiet, just talking in low voices. Were they speculating on where she was? The University rules said they were to wait fifteen minutes for a teacher to arrive. Then they could leave. She remembered she had not told them that rule.

"Good evening!" she said, breathlessly. She walked to the lectern and opened her briefcase, trying to be dignified.

She glanced up and saw Tyler's eyes upon her, with curiosity, perhaps a bit of concern. She remembered her haughty denial when he'd asked her, on the first day of class, whether she'd ever be tardy. She also remembered the time he, too, had been late.

"Well, I was wrong in what I said about my never being absent or tardy. I hope it won't happen again, but this," she said, with a glance at Tyler, "is tardy number one." He smiled slightly at her, surely recognizing his own words, and she had to smile back. Then she addressed the whole class. "Something unusual happened this evening. Part of a huge tree across the street from my house fell and blocked my driveway. I had to ask a friend to bring me here." She then proceeded with the class as she had planned.

During the break, to her surprise, Tyler approached her in the hall as she was returning from the restroom. "About that tree," he said. "I think I know about it." He pulled out his phone and showed her a picture on the screen.

She looked at it in surprise. "That's it, that's the tree that fell. It's across from the house where I'm living."

"My father just sent this to me. The woman whose property it's on has emailed our business and sent this picture. She wants us to come out and give her an estimate for taking the rest of the tree down as soon as possible. My dad will go there to give her one tomorrow. It sounds as if the tree is dangerous."

"The sidewalk goes right past it. And cars park on the street under it. If any more of it comes down, it could really injure someone. And it's so tall—if it fell, its top would hit my house."

"My dad will give her a fair estimate," said Tyler. "And we can take care of it. Too bad. It must have been a beautiful tree."

After class, he lingered after the other students had left. "Do you need a ride home?"

"No, a friend is picking me up."

"Good. I just wanted to be sure." Tyler walked off even as she tried to thank him.

Her heart was warmed by his offer. Was he being protective, thinking she might be stranded there in the evening without a ride on a campus where recently there had been a murder? Whatever his motive, she had missed a chance to know him better.

A few minutes later, she was waiting by the doorway of the Center when Henry pulled up. She opened the passenger side door and was getting in as Tyler's truck passed by. She hoped that he didn't see her. But at least, they had exchanged some words—and not just as teacher and student.

****

On Friday Tyler was eating his sack lunch with the crew at their work site when his father drove up, parked, and walked over to them. "I went over this morning and checked that huge magnolia the lady sent us the picture of. It's an emergency job. It needs to come down right away. The center has rotted out, and another limb could come down at any time. There's a road and sidewalk under the tree, and houses nearby could be impacted. I gave the owners the estimate and they've accepted."

"I'll call the city and get permission to close off the block," said Tyler, knowing his role. "Maybe we can start work on it late this afternoon."

He pulled out his phone, walked away from the men, tapped in the number. He explained the situation to the clerk, who said they'd call him back. In about an hour his phone vibrated. Tyler, up in the bucket, turned off his saw and put the phone to his ear. "We've issued the permit," the clerk said.

As Tyler pocketed the phone, he smiled slightly. He'd hoped to drive Ms. Holiday home last night—partly out of chivalry, but also perhaps to get to know her a little. That had not come about. But maybe, working across the street from where she lived, he would catch a glimpse of her. Maybe more.

****

Finally, she might have an opportunity to see Tyler outside of class. Early Friday morning before she left for her day classes, Katherine had seen a McHenry Tree Service truck come to the house across the street. The neighbors must have accepted the estimate, for when she got home late that afternoon, trucks were pulling up and orange cones were placed at either end of the block, along with signs saying "Road Closed." That evening a crew of men begin cutting the lower leafy limbs until darkness forced them to stop. She recognized Tyler among them.

On Saturday morning at eight a bucket truck pulled in, and, with a man standing in the bucket, safety chains attached to a belt on his waist, its crane began the ascent maybe sixty feet in the air, to the top of the tree. Although the man's eyes were covered with goggles and he wore a safety helmet, she recognized Tyler's build in the orange T-shirt, and the strands of his tawny hair sticking out. He was positioning the bucket using an instrument panel at its front, then reaching out with a chain saw and cutting off more leafy branches. They either fell to the ground, or he took them in hand and dropped them. Below, crew members picked them up and fed them to the growling chipper.

She had papers to grade, so turned away reluctantly and went to the back of the house. But she couldn't resist getting up periodically to check on the tree cutting process. From her front porch she had a good view—it was almost like watching a movie. The tree was now a naked skeleton, its heavy leaves and smaller branches gone. She saw Tyler turn off the chain saw, lower the bucket, and call out to a member of the crew, who tossed him up a plastic bottle of water. Tyler drank, then again raised the bucket high to the tree branches.

I shouldn't be watching him. He knows I live across the street. What if he sees me here, so unprofessional in these old denim cutoffs and this T-shirt, my hair down? Or maybe I want him to see me this way.

She made herself go back to paper grading.

When, a while later, she heard the sound of the machines become still, she went to the window. The crew was taking a break. The lowered bucket was back on its truck, and Tyler was sitting with the crew on the stone steps above the sidewalk across the street. They were eating lunch, and she could hear their masculine talk and laughter. One of the men looked older, maybe in his late fifties. She guessed he was Tyler's father.

Back at the kitchen table, grading again, she heard the machines start up and could not resist returning to the window. Tyler was back up in the bucket and within the huge, now bare tree limbs. The procedure was different now. The older man tossed him up a rope, aiming perfectly. Tyler effortlessly caught it, threw the rope over a limb, and secured it. He jerked the chain saw starter cord and, leaning out over the bucket, began sawing the limb. Soon it was severed and swinging by the rope. Slowly it was lowered, carefully so that it hit no wires.

With a *thunk,* the limb landed on the ground. The crew untied it, then rolled it to the curb before beginning the process all over again.

Katherine found herself nervously twisting a lock of hair around her finger and holding her breath for Tyler, up so high, leaning out like that with the heavy chain saw. But he seemed calm and methodical, moving from one limb to another. Wasn't it getting hot for him in the sun all those hours? The temperature, this Georgia spring day, was above eighty. She felt that he was doing most of the work, or at least the hard work, the work that took the most skill. Once a spray of sawdust hit him in the face, but he seemed unfazed. She went back to her papers.

By late afternoon, only the main trunk of the tree remained, like the tall mast of a ship. Standing at its base, the older man cut out a big wedge from one side. Then with the power saw he made a ring all around it, like a necklace. Tyler, up in the air, tied a rope around the trunk, and threw the other end down to the older man. Then Tyler pushed against the trunk as the older man and another crew member pulled on the rope. Nothing happened. Tyler pushed again. The long masthead-like column began to lean away from him—and within a few seconds had crashed to the ground. Katherine gasped, her hand on her heart. It was all over.

The rest was cleanup. The driver of the bobcat at first picked up the several large logs in its craw and tried to place them in the bed of a truck, but the logs were too big; some kept dropping out. The operator had to transport the big logs one by one—and then the smaller ones by twos or threes, into the truck.

When Katherine went back to the window after

eating a quick supper, she heard a roar of a gasoline blower and saw the youngest member of the crew, the blower attached to his back, clearing the sawdust out of the street. Tyler removed the cones and signs from each end of the block and put them in the truck with the logs. Finally, the older man and other crew members drove the bobcat and the chipper into the transport truck. They drove it and the truck with the logs away.

The street was quiet now. Only Tyler was left, and the bucket truck. Katherine lingered by the window, watching as Tyler took a towel from the cab of the truck and walked up to the house of the people he was working for. He stripped off his T-shirt. Katherine watched, riveted by the sight of his naked torso—his broad shoulders, his solid chest, his washboard flat abdomen. He picked up a hose and rinsed off his upper body and head, then toweled himself off.

Holding his towel and sweat-moistened work shirt, he walked back to the truck, threw them inside, then pulled out a white cotton Oxford-style shirt and put it on. Even as he buttoned it, he turned toward Katherine's house. She no longer cared how she was dressed. In fact, she was glad for him to see this side of her. As if drawn by an invisible magnet, she went out on the porch and down the steps.

She and Tyler walked toward each other, pausing when they came close. "Hello, Ms. Holiday."

"Tyler, you were amazing. That tree was so huge."

He looked at the giant, flat stump, a large hole in its center, its gnarled roots still clutching the earth. "It was probably close to two hundred years old."

She followed his gaze. "Yes." They were quiet a moment. Then she said, "There in that bucket, you made

45

taking it down look easy, graceful even, like a choreographed trapeze act I saw in Biloxi." She paused, then, embarrassed.

"My dad and I have been working together for years. We train the rest of the crew."

"You must not be afraid of heights."

Tyler laughed. "You can't be in this job. And we have a good team." He then became serious. "The view from up above was amazing. It would be even more beautiful now, with the sun setting."

She nodded, becoming aware of the neon-pink light in the western sky.

"I could take you up there with me in the bucket and show you."

"Wouldn't it be dangerous?"

"I'd put safety harnesses on us. Come on," he said. "Your neighbors went away for the day and night—they didn't want to be around for the cutting. I'll give you a quick ride before sunset."

She looked up at the glowing sky, mostly obscured by the neighborhood trees, then at him. This was a crazy suggestion—so unexpected. So exciting.

"All right," she said.

Tyler grabbed a tangle of harnesses from the back of the truck, then helped her up the steps of the truck onto an elevator platform, which carried them up to the bucket. He helped her into it, then climbed nimbly in behind her. Turning her to face the front, he stood behind her and fastened safety harnesses on each of them— around their waists, over their shoulders, between their legs. In the small bucket area, she had to stand close against him. She felt the hard warmth of his body.

"Ready?" he asked. She nodded. He pushed a button

on the instrument panel, and an engine at the side began to hum. He then moved a gear, and the bucket began to move outward over the street and to rise. Pressing closer against him, she gripped the sides.

"It's safe," he said. "Just look out at the view."

The bucket rose and rose. She looked down at her street, then at the grid of the neighborhood blocks as they came into view, then at the tops of the subcanopy trees. Above the ones forming the highest canopy, seventy feet in the air, the bucket stilled. She turned to the bright horizon of the west, shading her eyes as the sun sank lower behind the Piedmont foothills. Tyler's arms were on either side of her as he rested his hands on the instrument panel. "You like the view?"

"It's beautiful."

Then, quite suddenly, it seemed, the sun dropped out of sight behind the hills. Only a few pink luminescent clouds remained, suspended over the western horizon. She and Tyler watched as their light faded.

"We'll go down now," he said. He moved the gear on the panel, turned his head to look behind them, and guided the bucket on its long stem, like a dinosaur's neck, awkwardly lowering until it was folded back onto the truck. He unfastened the harnesses.

"Thank you, Tyler. It was…wonderful."

He steadied her lightly as she jumped on to the elevator platform, then hopped out himself. Leaving the platform, they went down the steps to the ground.

"You know, Ms. Holiday," Tyler said as he walked with her back to her porch, "it was against regulations to bring you up in the bucket. Only accredited personnel are supposed to go up." He paused. "Just like it's probably against regulations for University instructors to get too friendly with students in their class."

"It is," she said, feeling more bold. "If you can break a rule, so can I. Would you like to come in for a beer?"

"That may not be so wise. I am an owner of this tree business and owner of the bucket truck. I wasn't worried about breaking that rule tonight. I knew it was safe for you when I brought you up in the bucket. That's not the way it is with you and the University. And you don't know—" He hesitated.

"Know what?"

He smiled a little, as if joking. "Whether you'd be safe alone in your house with me."

For a moment she was taken aback. Was he referring to the murder? Then she said, "I'm not worried." She went up the steps to the porch of her house, and he followed. They paused in the darkness by her door. She thought again about his comment. "I—I'd just like to talk to you a little more about your writing."

"Oh, this will be another student-teacher conference?"

"We can think of it that way." Katherine opened the screen door. He followed her into the spacious entry hall, a beautiful staircase rising up to a second story on the far end. Katherine turned on more lights, displaying it all.

"This is quite a place!" Tyler said.

"I'm house sitting. This belongs to a professor in the English department and his wife. He has been teaching in England at the UGA at Oxford Study Abroad Program. They needed someone to stay in the house, keep the plants watered, take care of the cats, check the mail. And I have a place to live for a year rent-free."

"Sounds like a good deal."

"Come on to the kitchen." Katherine led him

through the hall to the back of the house. There on the kitchen table were stacks of student essays. Her supper dishes were in the sink. "You could call this my home office, I guess," she said. She opened the refrigerator and handed him a can of beer, then took one for herself. "Let's go out on the back porch."

Through the porch screens in the dusky light, they heard spring crickets chirping. She sat in a rocker and he sat on a futon couch across from her. They popped open their cans of beer.

"I don't understand why you're even in my course," she said. "You should have exempted English 101."

He shrugged. "I applied for admission late. I missed the placement exams."

"You're beginning work on a degree?"

"No. I'm just taking a class to please my mother."

"Ah yes, I remember her from your first essay," said Katherine.

"She's...dying."

"Oh, no!"

"She's been diagnosed with pancreatic cancer. I don't know how long she has. But she has always wanted me, her only child, to go to college. She was very disappointed when I decided to work with my dad instead. She's the intellectual, the college graduate. He's the physical man, out in the world, taking over his own father's business. When my mother learned her diagnosis, she started talking to me more than ever about going to college. She was so intense about it that I went to see about taking a continuing education class. I was late, but they let me register for this course. It's made her very happy. She thinks it means I'll go on for a degree." He tipped back his head and swigged some beer.

"I'm glad she is happy," said Katherine softly. "It was a beautiful thing for you to do." She listened to the crickets a moment, then spoke again. "About your writing, Tyler. You have a wonderful, original style. I think you could go somewhere with it. Have you thought of writing a novel, finding an agent?"

"I write just for myself."

"I could edit what you've done and help you find a place to publish."

"In your spare time?" He grinned and gestured toward the stacks of papers on the kitchen table.

"I'd make time."

"That woman poet in your class has already got dibs on you."

Katherine laughed. "I don't do well with poetry." Then she sobered. "I mean it, Tyler. You should do something with your writing."

"Now you remind me of my mother," he said. "With ambitions for me."

"I'd only want what you want." A thought struck her. "You must be hungry. Do you want some chicken salad? I have some left over from my supper."

"I need to get home." He put aside his empty beer can and stood.

Katherine rose as well. "There are only four weeks left in the semester."

"I know. I've been counting."

She walked with him to the front door and looked up at him—at his thick tawny hair, his blue eyes in his tanned face, and the darling creases in his cheeks when he was smiling, as he was now.

"You see," she said, "I was safe with you."

"I am not out the door yet."

Putting his hands on each side of her face, he bent his head and kissed her. It was just a quick kiss, but on the lips, and it held the promise of more. She could not help herself—with instinct as old as time, she closed her eyes, her lips beginning to part. But he moved away, pushed open the door, and was gone.

****

Tyler drove the big truck to his parents' house through the night. What an evening! It had gone beyond his wildest imaginings. As he worked that day, he'd caught glimpses of Ms. Holiday through the window of that big yellow house across the street, then a couple of times on the porch. He knew she was watching. Maybe that was why he lingered until all the crew had left. Up by the clients' house, he hosed off and put on a clean shirt. He looked across the street at Katherine's house, with lights now shining through the windows. She would be in there somewhere.

Then, the front door opened and she stepped out. She was not the Ms. Holiday of the classroom. That long hair, no longer in a bun, fell over her shoulders, and the T-shirt she wore revealed the outlines of her figure, always before mostly hidden under her high-necked sweaters and blazers. The cutoffs revealed her gorgeous legs. His breath was taken away at the sight as she walked toward him. When she said, "You were amazing," he knew for sure: he wanted her to be more to him than his teacher.

He knew also what he would do right then—offer to take her up in the bucket, show her the sunset. He thought she'd decline, but she actually accepted his offer. As the bucket rose, with her standing close against him, he was moved just by her nearness. Could she tell? Back on the ground, he reminded her of the rules about teachers not socializing with their students—even, trying to be honest, gave her an implicit warning about himself. But she asked him in for that beer anyway—it would be a kind of student-teacher conference, she said. And they had in fact pretty much kept their encounter in the house that way. Until he left. Then—he'd kissed her.

He pressed harder on the gas pedal. *Shit, it was just a brief, almost brotherly kiss, but I shouldn't have done even that.* Maybe he should stop attending her class. It was too late in the semester to withdraw; his grade would be a WF. But it wasn't the grade he cared about. It was not seeing her again. Of course, he would go back.

****

Katherine lay awake in bed that night, her hands clutching a pillow over her head. *Oh, my God, I've really messed up. When he kissed me, I should have been angry, told him to leave immediately. I'm disregarding all Dr. Flatt said at that meeting.*

She knew the truth, however. She'd wanted Tyler to kiss her. She'd wanted even more. There was no use even trying to deny her feelings now.

She worried all weekend about how to handle the situation when class met again. By Tuesday afternoon she'd decided what to do. In class she would focus on teaching, which she loved, and not think of him except as a student. She would try not even to look at him.

That evening she wore her most conservative "teacher" outfit—a black pinstriped pants suit, a turtleneck jersey, sensible heels. She kept her eyes down as Tyler came in and took his seat over on the far-left row. She noted Betty leaning over to him and asking a question. Then they were chatting together. She busied herself readying the overhead projector. Out of her peripheral vision she noted that Betty had leaned back into her place. In spite of herself, Katherine flicked her eyes over to Tyler. He was looking at her—and he winked. She smiled slightly.

Somehow, she knew then that everything would be all right. During the next four weeks, they would limit their relationship to the proper student-teacher roles. But surely they both knew there was something secret, magnetic between them—that, at the end of the semester, something would happen.

Chapter Four

At noon on the following Saturday, Katherine walked into the Hilltop Restaurant and spotted her two friends—Christy Ellis and her other former roommate, short, red-haired Marian McGuire, already in a booth. Marian, who sat facing the door, waved. Katherine waved back and went to the booth, where she slid in.

"Hi!" the two greeted Katherine, clasping her hands.

The waitress came by with her pad. "What can I get you besides water?" All three ordered white wine. After the waitress left, Katherine asked, "What's new with you two?"

"I still love my senior class at the academy," said Christy. "They're excited about going to college next year. Right now, they're working on their thesis papers."

"And I'm under some crazy deadlines at the *Banner*—one or two writing assignments every day," said Marian. "What about you?"

"Something very strange," said Katherine. She looked at her two friends—serious Christy and bouncy, excitable Marian. "You must promise to tell no one."

"Oh, we promise!" they exclaimed, leaning forward over the table.

"I have—maybe you'd call it a crush on a student in my evening composition class."

"What?" exclaimed Christy.

"He's about my age, he's smart, he writes

beautifully, and he's…well, sexy." Katherine paused. "And I think he likes me, too."

Marian's eyes glowed. "Have you seen him outside of class?"

"Just once. He owns a tree service with his father. They cut down a tree across the street from me. I asked him in afterwards for a beer." She paused. "We kissed."

Christy frowned. "Think of that murder on campus last semester. It might have been one of the teacher's students who did it. You were not very smart—or professional—to do something like that, Katherine."

"I know. That's why I don't want you to tell anyone."

"I think you'd better just get through the semester and forget him. I know it's been a long time since you've been with anyone. I'll fix you up with someone better than Spenser Johns."

Katherine drew in a breath. *I don't want any more 'fix-ups.'* "I shouldn't have told you about this."

Marian patted her shoulder. "That's okay, sweetie. We all get strange crushes sometimes."

"I'll stay away from him except as his teacher for the rest of the semester. And he'll stay away from me. He knows we have to do that."

The waitress returned with their wine. "Are you ready to order, or do you need a little more time?"

"Give us another minute or two," said Marian, and raised her wine glass in a toast. "To high school seniors, publishing deadlines, and—illicit relationships."

"Don't encourage her," said Christy.

After lunch, as Katherine drove out of the restaurant parking lot, Christy waved her down. Katherine lowered her window, and her friend leaned in. "I didn't want to say anymore at lunch—but be careful. I'm not saying this just because of that murder but because you might get in trouble professionally. Remember those two news stories we read about university professors who were suspended or fired because they tried to have some kind of relationship with a female student? The rules apply to women teachers too. And think of your parents."

Katherine felt irritated. Those cases Christy referred to seemed totally different from hers—male professors apparently preying on vulnerable young females, demanding sexual favors in return for good grades. In one of the cases, the female student herself reported the professor.

"I told you—until the end of the semester I will not see him except in the classroom."

Christy did not seem mollified. "I knew I'd been right to worry about you ever since Robert left for Texas. I admit introducing you to Spenser Johns was a mistake. But…getting involved with a student in one of your courses?"

"It's my *adult c*ourse," said Katherine sharply. Then she looked at her friend's concerned expression, and her tone softened. "If you met him, you'd understand."

****

Katherine lay on the examining table in her gynecologist's office, naked except for a thin paper wrap and the paper sheet over the lower half of her body. She hated waiting for the doctor to arrive—it seemed to take forever. And once they got her on the table, it was hard to go back to her purse and dig out her book to make time pass faster.

She was just about to do that anyway, sitting up and swinging her legs over the side, clutching the sheet to her, when the little knock came on the door and Dr. Moore, a middle-aged woman with graying hair, entered. "Hello, Katherine," she said. "How have you been?"

"Fine," said Katherine, lying back down.

Dr. Moore and her nurse adjusted the light, had Katherine put her feet in the stirrups, and proceeded with the exam. Katherine stared at the ceiling, trying not to be tense.

"All right, it's over," said Dr. Moore. "You can sit up now." She went to her file and looked it over. "Are you sexually active?"

Katherine hesitated. "I want to get back on birth control pills."

"Do you want the ones you were on…let's see, a year ago?"

"Yes."

Dr. Moore scribbled out a prescription. "You've gone almost a year without contraception."

"Yes." Katherine was tempted to explain that her old relationship was over, but that she might be in a new relationship and wanted to be prepared. But even though it was the truth, she was embarrassed. She was relieved that Dr. Moore did not question her further, but merely handed her the slip of paper to take to the pharmacy.

****

April was almost over. The final two writing assignments were argument essays—and for Katherine, this was the most difficult segment to teach. She wanted to choose controversial topics the students could become engaged in, at the same time avoiding ones that incited emotions rather than logic. During class discussions, she herself as moderator tried to remain neutral, merely pointing out fallacies or weak evidence. Likewise, she would judge their essays on the basis of how well they presented their views and provided rebuttals against opposing views.

For all three of her composition classes, the first topic assigned was whether or not capital punishment should be abolished. Their textbook included essays on either side of the case; she told them they were limited to those sources. Otherwise the issue of plagiarism yawned before her.

That topic proved successful. Only one strange thing occurred: when she pulled out Gene Whittaker's essay to read, an envelope fell out with her name on the outside. Curiosity tinged with a bit of dread, she opened it and found a poem, written in his far right-slanted, black-inked handwriting. The title was "Killing Me Sweetly."

Perhaps it was related somehow to the capital punishment topic, but intuitively Katherine felt it would be something inappropriate. She remembered a song with something like that title—about a young woman listening to a singer whose lyrics are so deep and personal that she feels as if he knows all about her personal life and emotions.

Would the poem suggest Gene knew something about her feelings—even the relationship between her and Tyler? Surely not. Or maybe the poem was saying that she was arousing feelings in him? Lord, she hoped not that either. Katherine glanced at the lines of the poem, and a few phrases jumped out at her: "Unheard melody…Strumming of blood…Sweet my pain…"

The theory that it was a student who had killed Dr. Morang passed through her mind, and she shivered a little. But of course, if the murderer was one of Dr. Morang's students, it could not be Gene. As a working non-traditional, he would not have been taking a day psychology course and Dr. Morang did not teach night courses—so he would have had no contact with her.

Katherine slid the sheet back into the envelope and wrote on the outside, "I'm sorry, but I do not feel qualified to critique student poetry. If you are interested in a course in creative writing, which includes poetry, I suggest applying to register for ENG 221."

She taped the envelope shut and went quickly on to his essay. Gene again had occasional brilliant phrases in his writing, but the ideas were not coherent, and his evidence more emotional than logical. She had to give it a C.

For the second argument essay, the morning composition classes were to argue for or against membership in sororities and fraternities. They could use personal experience as well as the essays included in the text as sources. But this topic would not do for her adult class. With them, she had decided instead to assign the question of gun control versus the rights of gun-owners. The evening they discussed the materials on both sides in the text and debated the issue, the students were sharply divided.

"I think it's dangerous for handguns to be carried in public at all," said Betty. "Guns should be left to the police. I agree with that chief justice, Warren Burger. The second amendment on the right to bear arms referred only to state militias, not to individuals."

James Waffle waved his hand to speak. "An essay in the textbook says that for more than two hundred years that's how federal courts defined that amendment."

Gene yelled out, "But they were wrong!"

Roy spoke up. "Yeah," he said. "The Supreme Court

ruled last year that the second amendment *does* guarantee the right of individuals to own and use weapons for self-defense in the home or place of business. And now a lot of states, including Georgia, allow people with permits to carry concealed guns in most public places."

Katherine was not surprised he was supporting Gene. He and Gene were friends—she knew they carpooled to the class.

Betty was still clearly upset. "The Court was influenced by the gun lobby. The National Rifle Association distorted the meaning of the second amendment just to sell guns. And now handguns are too easy for people to get and carry."

Carrie raised her hand. "One of the readings said applications for gun permits in Georgia went up almost eighty percent since that 2008 ruling about the meaning of the second amendment."

"Yes," said Betty. "So more people will get murdered with guns, like Dr. Morang."

Tyler spoke up. "Linguistic studies say the meaning of 'bear arms' in the framers' day was military. And the Court's ruling wasn't unanimous—it was five to four. The Court has overturned its rulings in the past—it has on school segregation or abortion. So in the future it might change that 2008 ruling."

"Bull!" Gene yelled out. "It won't ever change that ruling. In fact, gun laws are still too restrictive. People in every state should be allowed to own and carry any gun anywhere in public for self-defense—without having to apply and pay for a license or *permit.*"

Hubbub erupted from the rest of the students; Tyler turned in his seat to regard Gene. Betty cried out, "It's not the wild west anymore."

"Class! Gene!" Katherine said. "This is supposed to be a rational discussion."

As the students gradually quieted, Carrie said in a little voice, "At least most states don't allow guns on college campuses. They aren't allowed on campuses here in Georgia."

Gene was not finished. "Colleges have no right to make that restriction," he snapped. "I carry a gun. I need it for protection, and I need it as much on this campus as I do on the street. Like they say, only a good guy with a gun will stop a bad guy with one." He pointed at the class and then beyond them to Katherine, his mismatched eyes almost threatening. "Professor Morang was killed by a bad guy with a gun. If I'd been there with my gun, I might have stopped the killer."

Somewhat unnerved, Katherine said, "All right, we've discussed the issue enough. You all can present your views in your essays. But remember, you should not base your essay just on emotion. Your grade will be based on the quality of your writing, the evidence you give, which should include facts and quotes from the assigned reading, and logic." She looked at the clock. "It's time for a break."

Most of the students moved out into the hall. Gathering up her notes for that segment of the class, Katherine heard students still arguing. As Tyler passed her, also heading out into the hall, she nervously dropped the felt-tipped pen used to write on the overhead transparencies. It rolled across the table onto the floor.

He leaned over, picked it up and handed it to her. As before, he seemed to know how she felt. Perhaps he hoped to comfort her when he said, "No one will ever describe your class as boring, Ms. Holiday."

****

By mid-May, those last argument essays had been written and graded. Many of Katherine's students were against allowing handguns in public without restrictions. Most thought they should not be carried in government buildings, airport security checkpoints, or on college campuses. A few—including Gene and Roy—argued for full freedom in carrying guns. Katherine tried hard to be fair, not allowing her own views in favor of gun control to influence her grades. But Gene's paper consisted mostly of emotional assertions without the solid facts available in the textbook readings. Although some personal anecdotes he included were interesting in themselves, the essay also wandered, without clear structure. Once again, she had to give his essay a C.

On Tuesday of the final week of the course, Katherine cancelled class to hold individual conferences with her students. The conferences would start in mid-afternoon for those who could come in early, then run through the usual class time. She'd reserved a small study room for those conferences scheduled before the class period. The rest would be in the classroom. Each conference would last fifteen minutes. That wasn't much time, but she felt such individual meetings were valuable. She'd return their portfolios and discuss their overall writing progress, what their strengths were, where they could improve. This would help them write a better final exam essay.

Then, at the beginning of the Thursday session, they would write their evaluations of the class. After those forms were collected, she would end that last class of the semester by reviewing once again the elements of a good academic essay. She had given Tyler the sign-up sheet for individual conferences first—because of where he was sitting, she told herself. He had written his name in the last slot, after class from eight-fifteen to eight-thirty.

On Tuesday she was in non-stop conferences beginning at three-thirty; adrenaline kept her going. As she planned, she praised the students' strong points, but also discussed ways they might still improve—using more concrete examples with Carrie, avoiding certain grammar errors with Betty, the need for tighter organization with Roy.

Toward the end there was the conference with Gene. "I guess you just disagree with me about allowing guns on campus," he said wryly, looking at the grade of *C* on his last essay as she leafed through his folder.

"The grade is based on the quality of your argument, not whether I agree or disagree with you," she said. "In fact, you incorporated personal experience quite well. If you had buttressed your evidence with data and facts from the class readings and organized your argument better, the grade would have been higher." Leafing through his other essays, she reminded him again that he needed to use factual evidence, not simply go off on irrelevant, emotion-based digressions.

His lips twisted in his usual smirk. "You don't like digressions, Ms. Holiday? Digressions, *trans*gressions—they make life more interesting."

"We are talking about academic writing here…Mr. Whittaker."

Gene picked up his things to leave, but stopped by the lectern and looked down at her. "Is that why you wouldn't read my poem? It's not *academic writing*?"

She opened her mouth to respond, but, smiling that

strange smile, he turned and left. She was glad to call in the next student, who was waiting outside the door. This was her second to last conference, eight o'clock to eight-fifteen. She'd had no supper, barely time for a bathroom break.

The student was the short, pixie-like man. He was sweet and romantic and had wordy, flowery writing she'd tried all semester to modify, at least a little. For the conference, she had selected one of his paragraphs to compare to another on the same topic by a fellow student, but with a more direct, accessible style. "I don't want to change your personality," she told him. "But, as I've said before, in your college courses a simpler style like this one would be more appropriate—and communicate better."

The little man nodded with lowered eyes. His lips trembled a little.

"You have wonderful ideas," Katherine said, hoping she had not hurt his feelings yet again. "Just see, after you write the first draft of your final essay, which words you can leave out without losing your meaning."

"I'll try," said the little man. He stood up, not too steady on his feet.

"I've really enjoyed having you in class," she said, rising also and handing him his cane. "I think it's wonderful you've come back to school."

"Thank you." He picked up his portfolio and, leaning on his cane, shuffled through the door.

Perhaps she should not have tried to change his writing style at all, even if it would have helped him in his future classes. It seemed her suggestions had only depressed him. And how many more classes would he be taking, anyway? Teaching was sometimes hard.

She stretched. Now was the conference she'd been waiting for, but Tyler had not yet appeared. She walked out into the hall and looked toward the door to the outside. Suddenly someone came up the hall behind her and put strong hands on her shoulders. "Come on, get your things. I'm taking you somewhere else for our conference."

Startled, she turned. "Tyler! Where?"

"You'll see." He leaned against the door frame as she packed the few remaining papers in her brief case. She had been waiting too long for this. It seemed he had too. Besides, his essays were already wonderful—she did not need to give him advice.

They had not interacted in any personal way since that evening of the bucket ride and beer in her house—and the kiss. Now that the semester was virtually over, she had few qualms about what she was doing. Besides, just as when he came for a beer at her house, who would know about this? She switched off the classroom lights and walked beside him to the exit door.

"I hope you don't mind riding in my truck," he said. "I'll bring you back here to your car after our…conference."

"Of course, I don't mind."

Sitting beside him in the seat with her briefcase at her feet, Katherine was quiet, taking in the experience of the truck and of Tyler beside her. He, too, was quiet for a time, swinging the truck out into the street, then driving on to the Atlanta Highway, away from downtown and the bars where the students hung out.

Finally, he spoke. "So do you have a boyfriend, Ms. Holiday?"

She glanced sideways at him. "No."

He gazed intently out of the windshield, negotiating a lane change. "I saw someone picking you up outside of the Center that night the tree fell."

"That was my neighbor. Not a boyfriend." She paused. "What about you? Do you have a girlfriend?"

"No. Not right now." He looked over at her. His tone changed, became happy and light-spirited. "Have you ever been to Harry's?"

"Harry's?"

"It's a bar out past the bypass. They're having a good country band tonight. And it's not the type of place university people go." Even as he spoke, Tyler pulled in at a building that looked like large a fishing-cabin with a flashing neon sign: *Harry's Bar and Grill, Live Music Tonight*. Cars and pickups filled the parking area. Tyler turned off the ignition. "Do you like to dance?"

"I'm not a very good dancer."

"That doesn't matter. We're celebrating the end of the semester."

"Not quite the end."

"It's close enough." He got out of the truck, came around, and opened her door. He glanced down at her briefcase on the floor by her feet. "I don't think you'll need that."

"No," she said, getting out.

He smiled, the creases in his cheeks deepening, and escorted her inside. The space they entered was crowded and buzzed with chatter. The stage, at one side, was empty except for the instruments. The band was on a break. Tyler found an empty table in a corner. As they sat across from each other, he hailed a waitress and ordered a pitcher of beer. The girl delivered it promptly, along with two glasses. Tyler filled them and moved one of the glasses toward her.

Katherine took several swallows of the beer—she was really thirsty. Then, looking at him across the table, she said, "There's nothing I can suggest to improve your writing."

"I bet you can think of something."

She shook her head. "How old are you?"

"Does my age relate to my writing?"

"I just wondered how long it's been since you'd graduated from high school."

"Eight years."

That made him about twenty-six, she figured. "But you've been writing some since then?"

"When I have the time."

"What do you write?"

"Thoughts, descriptions, sketches—like the one you read about my mother. Fiction." He paused. "How old are *you*, Ms. Holiday?"

"I earned my master's degree in English at the University a year ago. I'm twenty-four."

"A good age." He saluted her with his mug and then refilled hers.

The band was starting up again. The music was so loud that it was impossible for them to continue the conversation. She was feeling relaxed now, uninhibited. She looked around at the others in the bar—the women's brief shorts and halter tops, the jeans and plaid shirts on the men.

"My clothes are out of place," she said, loud enough so he could hear over the music. She took off her blazer and unbuttoned the top few buttons of her blouse. Then she reached up, pulled off the band around her bun, and let her hair cascade over her shoulders.

Tyler looked at her, his eyes sparkling in the dim light. "You look ready to dance."

He stood, then pulled her to her feet. They went out to the dance floor. The music was fast, and she danced facing him, in thrall to the pulsating beat.

The next number was a slow one, one of those sad country love songs, and she and Tyler moved together wordlessly. She closed her eyes, felt his body against hers, and inhaled the scent of him. Perhaps it was shaving cream mixed with a faint scent of crushed leaves. Then something made her open her eyes. Over his shoulder she saw two students from her night class. Horrified, her heart skipped a beat. "Tyler, Roy Grant and Gene Whittaker are here."

He looked at the table she indicated. "Hell, I was sure we wouldn't see anyone we knew."

"They're watching us."

"We'd better go speak to them." He took her hand and led her to their table. "Hey," he said. "I thought Ms. Holiday should have a break after all those conferences."

The two at first seemed taken aback at Tyler's direct greeting, but then they looked with interest on this new version of their teacher. "What a way to get an *A,* McHenry," Roy said.

Katherine spoke up, trying to keep her tone light. "I may lower his grade—" she glanced up at Tyler "—if he doesn't dance well enough."

Gene regarded her, his eyes narrowed. "Just now, you *looked* like you'd give his dancing an *A double plus.*"

He might have been kidding, but she thought it held a suggestive—even hostile—undercurrent. Maybe she was the only one who felt it, for the other two laughed.

68

Tyler put his hand on the small of her back. "Well, see you in class on Thursday." He guided her back to their table, where he pulled out her chair, and asked, "When did you eat last?"

"Lunch at noon," she said.

He sat down and hailed the waitress. "What food do you have?"

"Hamburgers, pizza, French fries."

He looked to Katherine. "What do you want? You need to eat." Then, at her indecisiveness, "Bring her a burger and fries."

Katherine realized she did indeed need to eat and was grateful for the plate when it arrived. As she ate, a young male singer came out with the band and ran through a series of songs made popular by Hank Williams and Willy Nelson. She finished the food and mouthed, "Thank you," to Tyler.

When the singer left and the band began playing a slow song, Tyler said, "Another dance?"

"I don't know," said Katherine. "Gene and Roy—"

"Have left," he said. "Don't worry about them."

It was near midnight when Tyler got her back to her car, as promised. It was the only one left in the parking lot. "I'll follow you, make sure you get home safely."

"There's no need—"

"You were a little tipsy earlier," said Tyler. "And there's been that murder on campus. Drive slow."

She lived only a few blocks away and was soon parked in her driveway. Tyler pulled in behind her and came up to her as she got out of her car. He walked her to the door, then turned away.

"Good night," he said. "I enjoyed our…conference."

Chapter Five

On Thursday, the last meeting of the class, Tyler arrived only a few minutes before it was to begin. He pushed open the men's room door and went inside. At the urinal, he heard the door open and looked toward the sound. Gene had entered. Regarding Tyler, he broke into a smile. "Ah, hello there," he said. "So how was she?"

"Who?"

"Ms. Holiday. You and she were having a great time Tuesday night, weren't you? How was she?"

Tyler zipped up. "What do you mean?"

Gene lowered his voice. "Did you fuck her?"

Tyler took a threatening step toward him. "Watch your mouth."

Gene shrugged and held out his hands. "Sorry. I just wondered, that's all. So prim and proper and know-it-all in the classroom...But I bet she was good."

Tyler slugged him.

Gene fell back, held his mouth for a moment, then dropped his hands and looked again at Tyler, his small eyes alight. "Oh, sensitive about that, are you?"

And suddenly, he struck at Tyler's jaw with his fist. The two began grappling with each other, knocking back against the sinks, then against the stall doors.

They heard a *whish* as the door to the hall opened. Roy entered. "Hey!" he said. "Ms. Holiday wants you both to come to class. We're doing the end of the semester evaluations."

The two men broke apart. Tyler glared at Gene, then looked to Roy. "We're coming."

They filed out the door. From the corner of his eye, Tyler noted Katherine sitting in a chair in the hall, as she was apparently supposed to while the class wrote out their evaluations. He did not look directly at her. He walked into the classroom, ahead of the other two.

****

On that last meeting of the evening class, Katherine watched the students as they came into the classroom. Following departmental directions, she would hand out the class evaluation forms and ask one of the students to collect them and turn them in at the night school office. She herself was supposed to wait outside the classroom. The forms had some objective questions on which the students were to rank her on a scale of one to five, and then a space for a written comment. No matter how well her classes seemed to have gone, she was always a little nervous about the evaluations.

By six-thirty all the students had settled in their seats except for Gene and Tyler, who were missing.

"Maybe they're in the rest room," said Maureen, seeing her note the empty seats.

"We need to start the evaluations." Katherine handed out the forms and gave the manila envelope containing them to Betty, the girl who sat across from Tyler. "Will you collect the forms and turn them in to the office when everyone is finished? You can give Gene and Tyler the last two when they come in."

Betty nodded and took the envelope.

"These evaluations should take about fifteen minutes," Katherine told the class. She walked out into the hall and sat down in a chair against the wall, leaving the classroom door open.

The corridor was empty. Hoping to divert herself, she began looking at the notes she had brought out with her. Then she heard loud voices from the men's restroom and some thumps. She stood. The voices had ceased, but the thumps were getting louder. She peeked into the classroom.

"Roy!" She motioned to him. He came out to her. "Would you check the men's restroom? Something is going on in there."

He hurried to the rest room door and went inside. After a moment, the thumps ceased. Finally, the door opened, and Tyler, Gene, and Roy came out. There was some blood at the side of Gene's mouth, and he had a lump on his forehead. A bruise was beginning to form on Tyler's jaw, and he was flexing his hand. All three entered the classroom. Tyler and Gene did not look at her, but Roy did as he passed.

"Thank you," she whispered.

With a silent nod, he took his seat.

Katherine's mouth felt dry as dust, her hands frigid as ice cubes. Obviously, Tyler and Gene had been fighting. Why? The evaluations seemed to take forever. Surely fifteen minutes were up. Finally, Betty emerged from the classroom with the manila envelope and went down the hall toward the evening class office.

She entered the totally silent classroom. Glad that Gene, with that blood drying on his mouth, sat at the back, out of the students' line of vision, she began automatically reviewing once again the elements of a good essay. Then on the overhead projector she showed excerpts from the last set of essays, which they discussed. The atmosphere was becoming normal again. The class even shared a few laughs. Finally, the discussion was over. Katherine wished them luck on their take-home exam and dismissed them early. Students clustered around her lectern, saying goodbye. Gene and Tyler exited the room.

Once all the students had gone, Katherine slowly packed her briefcase. For the last time, she switched off the lights in Classroom Six and walked out into the hall. What could she do but go home? Out in the parking lot, in the soft May dusk, she saw a figure leaning against her car. He seemed to be studying the ground at his feet. Was this someone she should be afraid of? She slowed as she came closer. The person waiting there lifted his head. She let out a breath of relief. It was Tyler.

Standing before him, she could see, even in the dim light, the bruise on his jaw. She touched it lightly. "Tyler, what happened between you and Gene? Was it about Tuesday night?"

He shrugged. "It doesn't matter. He said something that he shouldn't have, that's all."

"Oh, Tyler, I'm sorry."

"It wasn't your fault. It was mine. I didn't think we'd see anyone who knew you at Harry's. But I should have made myself wait to take you out until the semester was really over."

She clicked her car key twice and heard the locks on all the doors pop up. "Get in the car," she said. "I'll drive this time."

He did as she said. She drove the few blocks to her house, then turned off the ignition and looked at him. "I told you before—I'm not afraid to be alone in the house with you."

"And I told you maybe you should be." He leaned over the console, gently turned her face to him, and really kissed her this time. She pressed toward him. This kiss was all she had imagined it would be.

After long delicious moments, Katherine and he got out of the car. She unlocked the door of the house and they went inside. A loud meow was heard, and two black and white furry creatures rushed to her. "I need to feed the cats," she told him. He followed her into the kitchen and watched as she dumped kibble into their food dishes and gave them fresh water.

Then she turned to him. "You should put some ice on that bruise."

"That's not a priority," he said. "Feeding the cats was. Now this is." He took her to him and kissed her as he had in the car.

After some time, she asked, breathless, "Are you working tomorrow?"

"I don't think so. The forecast says rain."

"Then you can stay awhile."

"If it suits you."

"It suits me."

She moved toward the bedroom she used while house sitting for the Fosters. The lights were off, and she did not turn them on. Facing Tyler by the bed in the dark, she reached up and slid her hands under his shirt, wanting just to feel him. And then his hands were upon her too, loosening her hair, sliding her blouse down her shoulders. Katherine soon learned why she was supposed to be afraid of being alone with Tyler in the house. It was a wonderful experience.

Afterward, he sat up and turned on the small lamp beside her bed. Looking down at he said, "You're as beautiful without your clothes as I thought you'd be."

"When were you thinking of me without my clothes?"

"All the while you were teaching."

"You were not! You were listening to me. You were thinking about writing."

"I can multi-task."

She laughed. "I'll have to remember what you were thinking when I grade your exam."

"You'll take off points for my thoughts?"

"Maybe I should."

"You should take those thoughts as a compliment. And you have something to confess to me, too, Ms. Holiday."

"What is that?"

"You thought I'd plagiarized my first essay."

She looked at him, surprised he had brought it up. "You should take *that* as a compliment," she said.

"I will." He leaned over her to kiss her again.

****

The following week the students submitted their take-home exams by email attachment. She read them and turned in her final grades at the registrar's office on a rainy, windy Friday. Most of her evening class students had received *A*'s or *B*'s. Gene's average was a *C*. Even on his exam, his ideas bounced all over, even more than they had in his work throughout the semester.

She was always relieved to have her grades turned in, but there was an additional reason for her relief this time. Now that the semester was truly over, she could see Tyler, not as his teacher, but as…what?

She had not heard from him for a week—since the Thursday night they'd made love. She began to worry.

Would he disappear into his own world, which was so far apart from hers? Now that their unspoken expectations been realized, had he lost interest? He did not call her even over the weekend.

On Monday, she received a phone call from the head of the English department. "Ms. Holiday?" Dr. Flatt said. "Could you come in to see me sometime this week? I need to confer with you about something."

That took her by surprise. "Why, yes."

"Could you come at ten tomorrow morning?"

"Of course." She wanted to ask why, but something in his tone kept her from doing so. Her contract as an instructor ran for three years, so she had two more years to go. This meeting should not be about her job.

At ten o'clock the next morning, dressed in a prim skirt and cotton pull-over top, her hair in its bun, she appeared in the English department office. "I'm Katherine Holiday," she told the secretary. "I have an appointment with Dr. Flatt at ten."

"Oh yes, Ms. Holiday. You can go on in." The woman indicated the adjoining office.

Katherine walked hesitantly up to the door. The large man at the desk looked up at her standing there. "Ah, Ms. Holiday, come in," he said. He seemed slightly uncomfortable. "Have a seat."

She smoothed her skirts behind her and sat down in the chair on the other side of his desk, looking at him questioningly.

When he pulled out a manila envelope, her heart began to race. She recognized the envelope in which her evening class evaluations had been placed. "Your evaluations, both in the day classes and the evening class, were quite good," he said. "But I wanted to ask you about one of them."

"Oh?" was all Katherine could manage.

Dr. Flatt put on reading glasses. "This particular evaluation includes quite a lengthy description of—well, your relationship with another student in your evening class. I reminded you all at the beginning of the semester—it is University and departmental policy that instructors do not socialize with their students, especially those of the opposite sex, in a…familiar way."

"Yes."

"This student's evaluation describes you going with a male student in the class to a bar. It says that you were drinking. It describes your dancing with him in a, well, intimate way." He looked up at her. "This does not sound good, Ms. Holiday."

Katherine took a deep breath. "None of the other students said anything like that, did they?"

"No," said Mr. Flatt. "But you are a young woman—like that professor who was murdered on campus, possibly by one of her students. Especially in an evening class of adults, you need to be circumspect."

"Circumspect?"

"Watchful and discreet; cautious; prudent."

"Yes, of course."

"He gave names," Dr. Flatt said.

"He? The person who wrote the evaluation was male?"

"He sounds male. He said you were dancing at a bar named Harry's with a Tyler McHenry. Do you deny it?"

Katherine looked down. "No," she said. Then she looked up. "The semester was almost over. I was supposed to have a conference with Tyler. We decided to have it somewhere other than in the classroom."

"In Harry's Bar?"

She did not answer.

"I looked up Mr. McHenry's grade. I see he received an *A* in the course."

"He is an excellent writer," she said.

"Hmm." Dr. Flatt looked at her over his spectacles. "All your other evaluations were quite positive. You sound like an outstanding teacher. And apparently there was no danger to you from Mr. McHenry. Still, you were violating departmental policy. It's clear you had an instance of bad judgement."

"Yes," said Katherine.

"I assume you will not do anything like that again."

"I don't think those circumstances will ever come up again, Dr. Flatt."

"Then I will redact the names and other specifics in this report," he said . "But I think next semester it will be best if you teach all four of your classes during the day— no adult evening class."

Katherine nodded. "I understand."

The man stood and extended his hand. She took it. At the door she paused and turned back to him. "Tyler McHenry will not get in any trouble for this, will he?"

"No," said Dr. Flatt. "I think the situation has been taken care of here today."

"Thank you," said Katherine.

She left the office and the building in a kind of numb haze. Then in her car, anger overtook her. *That damn Gene. He wrote that evaluation—after Tyler and he fought in the rest room. He was getting back at Tyler— and me.* She would never tell Tyler about Gene's evaluation. She'd seen that Tyler had a temper. She was afraid of what he might do.

Tyler called her that night. "Hello, Katherine." She'd recognize that voice, that soft accent anywhere. Your grades are in, aren't they? We can go out any place we want to now."

"Yes," she said.

"I want to take you out on a real date. A nice dinner. Can I pick you up tomorrow at seven?"

"Yes."

"I'll see you then."

It wasn't all over.

****

"So you've got a dinner date tomorrow and can't eat with us?" Tyler's mother, lying on the couch that evening, said. "Who is *this* girl?"

Tyler felt embarrassed. His mother had never approved of the girls he took out. Of course, she seldom met them. He'd barely mentioned Katherine to his mother, but she'd picked up on it right away. He had to tell her. "She was the instructor of that college course I was taking."

His mother raised herself up against the cushioned arm of the couch. "That composition course?" He nodded. "Well," she said. "That's a change for you. So, maybe at last you've found someone worthy of you. I want to meet her, Tyler."

"It's too soon, Mom. We're just getting to know each other outside of class."

Her gray eyes bored into his. "I don't have much time, Tyler. I want to talk with her while I still can."

"I'll see," said Tyler. He paused. "Okay, when we go out to dinner tomorrow, I'll ask her to come here sometime and meet you."

"Good," said his mother. "Sometime soon."

****

Tyler took Katherine to the Five and Dime, a restaurant run by a famous chef in an old house on Milledge Avenue. They sat in a booth in a corner, looking at each other in the flickering candlelight. He wore a navy-blue sport coat and tan slacks. His thick hair seemed a bit more bleached by sun, and there were white circles in his tan face where his goggles must have rested. She wore a long skirt with a split in it, a slightly off-the-shoulder blouse, hoop earrings. Her hair, long and shiny, was down over her shoulders.

Before dinner, she had a daiquiri; he had a scotch. He raised his glass. "To us."

"To us," she said. They touched glasses, and she sipped her tangy drink. "I was afraid there might not be any 'us.' "

"Why?"

"When I hadn't heard from you all week."

"I'm sorry, I should have called sooner. But I thought you'd know I'd call." He put his hand over hers. "You were busy grading exams. I wanted to wait until the class was officially over. I didn't want you to be in the 'Ms. Holiday' role anymore." He paused. "And on Friday there was a mini-tornado in Winterville that took down a lot of trees. I was in the bucket all weekend."

"You are like a doctor, on call."

He laughed. "I guess it is a little like that. They do call us tree doctors sometimes." Then he sobered. "There was another reason I didn't call. My mother's condition is getting worse."

"Oh, no!"

"I've told her about you. She wants to meet you."

"I'd like to meet her."

"I'll set something up soon."

After dinner, back at her house, Katherine touched his jaw. "Your bruise is healing."

"I'd forgotten about it."

"I'm glad."

"Don't think I've forgotten about Gene, though," he said. "I better not ever run into him again."

"He works in the appliance department of Howe's Home Supplies," she said. "Stay away from there."

Tyler laughed then buried his lips in her neck. And they both forgot about Gene.

****

Tyler took her to meet his mother the following Sunday at his parents' home in the tiny rural community of Farmingdale, about half an hour south of Athens. They lived in a late nineteenth-century farmhouse on a lot bordered by pastures where cows grazed. A large shed and a somewhat dilapidated doublewide sat at the back of the lot.

"That's where we keep our equipment," Tyler said, pointing to the shed. "And that"—he gestured toward the doublewide—"is where I live. Come on, you might as well see it. It's nothing like the house you're staying in."

She climbed up the three steps to the flimsy little door, and, ahead of him, entered a small living room with mottled wall-to-wall rug, a couch, recliner, and television. A coffee table by the couch was piled high with papers and books, a laptop in the only bare spot. A small kitchen with the bare essentials—stove, sink, refrigerator—was off to one side. Beyond that was a narrow hall that must have led to a bedroom and bath.

"Well," he said, as she silently regarded the scene, "this works for me for now."

"You do your writing here?" asked Katherine, indicating the coffee table.

"I do." He opened the laptop, touched a few keys, and a document with double spaced printing came up. "Here's what I'm working on. It's a novel about a father and son."

"Inspired by 'Indian Camp'?"

"Not really. I've been working on it for a while. It's just something that came to me."

"I'd love to read it."

"I need to do some more work with it. Then if you still want to…"

"I'm not teaching this summer. I have lots of time." She looked at his kitchen area, with dishes piled high in the dish rack. "Do you cook?"

"Not much. I eat with my parents a lot of the time. You wouldn't expect me to be a gourmet cook, would you? My specialty is more like macaroni and cheese out of a box."

She laughed. "And your bedroom is down there?" she asked, looking toward the hall.

"You may get to see that another time."

"May?"

"*Will*." He took her arm. "Come on to the house. My mother is waiting."

They walked across the lawn and entered the back door. They walked through a hallway where various jackets and work boots were stored and into a large kitchen where Katherine saw and smelled coffee brewing in a coffee maker. "Mom?"

"In here, Tyler." The voice was deep and rasping. They entered a sort of living room or den. A long, bony, gray-haired woman was lying on the couch, a blanket over her lower body, her head on a pillow. Her face turned toward them, her sharp flint-colored eyes appraising Katherine. The woman did not wait for an introduction. "Ah, so this is Ms. Holiday. You look too young to be a college professor."

"Not a professor, Mrs. McHenry, just an instructor." Katherine held out her hand, and the woman took it.

"Yes, the class was a basic composition course, wasn't it? Tyler really didn't need that."

"That's what I told him," said Katherine.

"Tyler, why don't you go out to the shop and find your father and bring him back here," said the woman. "In the meantime, Ms. Holiday and I can talk. Then we can all have some coffee."

Tyler looked to Katherine. She nodded.

He then gave his mother a look that suggested a bit of worry, and perhaps a bit of warning. "I'll be back in a few minutes." Then he turned and left.

Katherine sat down in a nearby upholstered chair. "I'm sorry you're not feeling well."

"It's more than not feeling well," said the woman. "I am dying. And I want to see Tyler taken care of before I go. He is a very intelligent young man, Ms. Holiday. He could have been valedictorian of his high school class if he'd tried. He was too much of a free spirit. Still is."

"Is it bad to be a free spirit?"

"If it ruins your potential, it is. I had always assumed any child of mine would go to college. But of course, I married someone very different from me. I was young, just out of high school. My parents called him a redneck. Well, I guess he was. A redneck tree cutter working for his father." A slight smile touched her lips for the first time. "He was very handsome." She stopped smiling.

"My parents saw to it that I got a college degree anyway, but they were right. My life did turn out quite different from what I expected. And now my husband has turned our son into a redneck tree cutter as well."

"Tyler is a skilled professional arborist," Katherine said. "I've seen him work. And I think his writing shows a kind of genius. Of course, I understand how you feel about college, but Tyler could be a famous novelist without taking another college course. Neither Hemingway nor Faulkner had college degrees."

"Ah, you speak out of infatuation," replied the woman. "But perhaps I can turn your infatuation into an advantage for me, because I think he is quite taken with you as well. It is much more important to have a college degree now. I think you can see that he continues in a degree program. You can make sure he sticks with it."

"What kind of degree do you picture him getting?"

"I can see him in the humanities—history, literature, philosophy. I tried to share my background in those subjects with him. I, too, was an English major, Ms. Holiday."

"Please call me Katherine."

"Katherine." The woman's voice intensified. "The work Tyler does is dangerous. A limb fell on his father while he was doing that kind of work. It broke his hip. Now Tyler has to do most of the hard work. He is young and strong now, but he can't keep it up forever. And someday he may be hurt too." She paused and seemed to try to calm herself, to speak rationally. "He'd be eligible for Georgia's HOPE scholarship, the UGA honors program. He can work with his father part-time to make some money if he needs to. Then when he gets his degree, he wouldn't have to do that anymore. Will you help me? Will you keep him in school? I won't be here to do that."

Katherine spoke gently. "You said Tyler is a free spirit, Mrs. McHenry. Free spirits know what they want to do. In the end, what Tyler does with his life will have to be his decision."

"You can *help* him decide." The woman sat up and turned to her, her eyes flashing. "You are the first girl I've met who could do this. The others—they didn't care about college either. And I knew they were just temporary. I think you will be different. I wish I could have waited to tell you all this until you and Tyler had been together longer, but I haven't much more time."

Katherine heard the back door open, then male voices. She touched the woman's hand. "I promise I'll try to do whatever is best for Tyler."

Katherine looked up as two men entered the room. What she saw took her breath away. Two such handsome men, Tyler of course, in his open necked shirt and blue jeans, and an older version of Tyler, heavier, with more creases in his face and strands of gray in his hair—but he had the same blue eyes, tan skin, and muscular build. As they approached, she noted that the older man was limping.

"Katherine, this is my father," Tyler said. "Dad, Katherine Holiday."

The older man extended his hand. She took it, feeling its strength and warmth—like Tyler's. "I saw you from a distance when you and Tyler and your crew took down that old magnolia on Dearing Street," she said.

"Yes, that was quite a tree," replied the man. "So…you were Tyler's teacher."

"Technically yes, but I'm not sure how much I

taught him that he didn't already know."

The man's eyes twinkled. "I don't think he feels his time was wasted."

"Well, everyone sit down," broke in Tyler's mother. "Tyler, go bring the coffee from the kitchen. I have cups and saucers here already."

Tyler went to fetch the coffee, and Katherine, seeing the tray with the cups on a sideboard, brought it over to the coffee table. She took the carafe from Tyler when he returned and poured everyone a cup. Sugar and cream were also on the tray. When everyone had fixed their coffee, they sat silent for a moment.

"Katherine, how did you come to be teaching at the University?" his mother asked.

"I earned a master's in English there a year ago. At that time there was a big surge in the number of students attending the university—and the department needed more instructors to teach the introductory composition and literature courses. They gave me a three-year instructorship."

"You like teaching in college?" the woman asked.

"I love it."

"What will you do when your contract is up?"

"She probably doesn't know yet, Mother," Tyler said.

"I'm sure she has some idea."

"Perhaps I will go on for a PhD in English," Katherine said.

"Oh my! A doctorate! Very impressive. I should have done something like that."

There was an awkward moment of silence. Then Mr. McHenry spoke up. "Katherine, have you ever gotten out to see Oconee Forest during your time in Athens?"

"No, what is that?"

"It's land on the Oconee River owned by the University. They've made it into a sort of arboretum, with many specimen trees. Tyler and I have done some work there. You should go hiking there with him sometime."

Katherine looked at Tyler. "I'd like that."

"Sundays would be the best day," said the man. "We don't usually work on Sundays except in cases of emergency, but Tyler and I have been working six days a week lately. He's more than my right-hand man now. I couldn't run the business without him."

Katherine's voice was soft. "I saw that."

Tyler stood. "Hey, Mom, you get some rest."

Katherine and he gathered the cups, saucers, and the coffee carafe and returned them to the kitchen. Katherine went to the sink to rinse out the dishes and put them in the dishwasher, but Tyler laid a hand on her arm. "My dad will do that."

They went back to the den. "See you later, Mom and Dad."

"It was nice to meet you both," Katherine said.

"Nice to meet you too, little lady," replied Tyler's father.

His mother spoke from the couch. "Remember our conversation." She looked intensely at Katherine for a moment, then rested her head back on the pillow and closed her eyes.

Chapter Six

In his truck after the visit with his parents, Tyler said, "Let's go to your house and you can change to your hiking clothes. We can go to Oconee Forest this afternoon."

Katherine looked at his hands on the wheel, strong, competent, and rather wished they could just go to her bedroom. But maybe after their visit to the forest... "All right."

After a quick change of clothes, she returned to his truck. Before long, she found herself hiking along a narrow trail behind Tyler, with trees towering above them. "That's a butternut hickory," he said, indicating the tree they were passing. "Its leaves turn a bright yellow in the fall... That one is a southern sugar maple— it's an understory tree. This is *Ulmus rubra*, red or slippery elm, a canopy tree—see how high it is? This type has survived the Dutch elm disease that has taken out most of the American elms... There's a White Oak. I think it's the most beautiful of the oaks. Did you know their wood makes the absolute best lumber for siding barns?"

"You love the trees, don't you? And know them well."

"I know our Piedmont trees."

"The university has a good school of forestry."

"Ah, I can tell my mother has talked to you," said

Tyler. "Let's sit down." They settled on a grassy knoll under the elm tree. Tyler stretched himself out. Reaching over, he pulled her closer to him.

"Your mother worries that your work is dangerous," Katherine said. "She wants me to encourage you to go to college and get a degree in the humanities."

Tyler laughed. "She's been encouraging me to do that for years. But our work is not as dangerous as she thinks. My father and I and most of the crew are certified by the ISA, the International Society of Arboriculture. We're well trained and follow the safety procedures. We haven't had any serious accidents for years. Dad's was very unusual." He looked at Katherine's expression. "Besides, many professions are dangerous—fighting fires, enforcing the law, farming, serving in the military. Accidents—equipment malfunction, a slip of the hand, human error—can happen in any situation." He took her hand. "Even teaching can be dangerous. You might run into a problem student, even a crazy one. Maybe that's how that woman professor was murdered on campus. It's better not to think about negative things, Katherine. Best just to do what you love."

She lay beside him and rested her cheek on his chest. "You're right, I know. But I have to ask—have you considered doing some other type of work?"

"I love *this* work. It's exhilarating to be up in the bucket or harness, in the branches sometimes seventy feet above the ground—like a trapeze artist. You saw that when I took you up in the bucket, didn't you? You said what we did reminded you of the aerial act in Biloxi. I like the challenge of cutting trees safely and well, working with ropes and tie knots and rigging limbs to be lowered to the ground. And what we do is important.

You know from the tree near your house—when trees are dead or dying, they can be a serious hazard—they need to be taken down." He paused, then went on. "But taking down trees isn't all we do. We trim trees to keep them healthy and safe. As you said—it's like being a doctor. And it's also like being an artist. I love seeing a tree that I've worked looking beautiful—and natural. And in my case, there's family tradition. My grandfather, my father's father, was an arborist who started the McHenry Tree Service. My father took over his business, and now I'm part of it too."

Hearing the passion in his voice, she looked at the leaves above them. They were beautiful with the sunlight filtering through. She felt his hand on the back of her neck, a warm caress.

"So what do you think, teacher?"

"I told your mother it was your decision. That I wanted what would make you happy. Your work is important—and obviously makes you happy." She pulled back and looked at him. "But you do work such long hours, Tyler. What about your writing?"

"I write at night."

"How many hours do you write?"

"I don't count. The hours slide by. Suddenly, I look up and realize it's time to sleep. But by day I want to do the work I do."

"You've convinced me. I'm proud you're an arborist." Katherine leaned over and kissed him. Then she straightened up with new resolve. "But you must let me read your novel when it's finished, Tyler. Knowing how you write, I'm sure it should be published."

****

So she really wanted to read his novel.

Tyler sat at the coffee table and pulled it up on the laptop screen. He wanted to give her a hard copy as he had with his essays in class, and his rickety old printer might just be able to print it out without dying. But he still felt reluctant for anyone to read it. It wasn't ready yet, was it? What if she didn't like it?

He scrolled through the manuscript, re-reading, typing in changes. If he wanted anyone to read his work, it would be Katherine. His father was not a reader, and his mother was too sick. His high school English teachers were overworked with their own classes, and anyway, he hadn't been in touch with them for years. Yes, it had to be Katherine. And he wanted it to be.

He pulled up the print menu on the screen, clicked on the print order. The old machine in the corner of the living room area coughed to life and began slowly, one by one, spitting out pages.

****

Katherine was going down the steps from the University library. It was a late afternoon in early June, and she had been reading some articles in academic journals about the teaching of composition, thinking already of the fall semester.

"Hello, Ms. Holiday."

She saw the thin, dark-haired young man with slightly crossed eyes climbing the steps toward her—Gene. She spoke coldly. "Don't speak to me as if you hadn't done anything."

He tilted up his head to look at her, shading his eyes from the afternoon sun. He still had a slight mark on the side of his mouth from the fight in the restroom. "What do you mean?"

"You know very well what I mean."

He began to smile. "You've gotten back your evaluations already?" She began to move past him, not replying, but he must have recognized affirmation in her response. He grasped her arm. "You don't know what you're talking about. The evaluations are anonymous."

"I didn't need a name."

"Oh." He smiled fully then. "Did you get in trouble because of an evaluation?"

She jerked her arm away and rushed off down the wide sidewalk toward the parking lot. Her heart pounded with repressed rage. It was because of him that she wouldn't get to teach an adult class next year, and she'd loved working with those non-traditional students. In fact, because of him, she could have lost her entire instructorship.

She slowed to a more normal walking pace. At least any more encounters with Gene were unlikely. Since she would no longer be teaching in the Continuing Education Center, she would probably never see him again.

****

Tyler's truck pulled into her driveway around seven o'clock that evening. She saw him from the front porch, where she had been sitting watching for him. She descended the steps and ran to embrace him as he got out of the truck

"Hey, watch out. I've come directly from work," he said. He had obviously not had a chance to hose off as he had when he'd worked across the street. His shirt still had dark patches of sweat under the arms, across his back, on his chest.

"I don't care."

"All right, then." He put his arms around her, pulled her close, and kissed her for a long minute. Then, stepping back, he held up a manila envelope. "I've brought you my novel."

She took it from him. "I can't wait to read it. I'll read it tonight."

"How about tomorrow? There's other things we can do tonight."

She looked at him, then smiled. "Come on in. You need a shower."

"I've got a change of clothes in the truck." He reached back for his clothes, and the two of them crossed the lawn and entered the house. Katherine closed and locked the door.

Tyler peeled off his clothes in her bedroom. As she looked at his smooth skin and sculpted muscles in the light of the setting sun coming through the windows, she thought of Michelangelo's *David.* She'd seen it when she visited Florence with her parents years ago. Then a young, innocent girl, she'd been fascinated with the beautiful nude marble figure, with the parts of male anatomy she had never seen. Now even more fascinated with this living figure, she had to make herself turn away.

"I'll get some towels and start the shower for you."

He came into the bathroom as she was reaching into the shower stall to test the temperature of the water. "I think after that hug, you'd better come in with me."

He took hold of her, expertly pulling her shirt off over her head, unhooking her bra and dropping it to the floor. Stepping backwards into the shower stall, he began to pull her in with him, her old cutoffs still on. Breathless, laughing, she flipped off her sandals just before he lifted her under the cascading water.

Sometime later they sat side by side on the futon on the back porch drinking beer and eating the pizza she had heated in the oven. They were clean and soap-fragrant in fresh clothes, their hair still wet. They finished the entire pizza. It had tasted wonderful.

Love, Katherine thought, enhanced one's appetite. But she had something she wanted to talk to Tyler about, and she turned to him. "Tyler?"

"Yes?"

"I'll have to leave this house at the end of the summer sessions. Dr. Foster and his wife will be coming back early in August. I'll try to find an apartment. Normally I'd look for one or two roommates, but now, I want privacy…for us."

Tyler put his arm around her. "You have nearly two more months here, anyway. I guess apartments near the campus are expensive." He removed his arm. "Maybe I'm not so good for you. You might be better off with a college professor. Or that lawyer neighbor of yours."

Katherine shook her head. "*You* are good for me."

They were quiet for a few moments before he spoke again. "You've met my parents. Tell me about yours."

"My father taught English at Colgate, a little college in upstate New York. He thought I'd stay in New York state for grad school, but Christy Ellis, a good friend of mine, had relatives in Georgia and was applying to UGA so I applied—and they gave me a teaching assistantship. So I came to Georgia."

"And your mother?"

"She met my father in college. She was the traditional housewife. Still is. Loves to garden and cook."

"And which one are you more like?"

Katherine smiled. "I think I'm like both of them. They both doted on me, their only child."

"Your parents got along well together? They had a happy marriage?"

"A very happy marriage." She looked at Tyler. "What about your parents?"

"They decided to marry when she got pregnant with me—not long after they met. They probably shouldn't have married. I never knew my mother to be happy. There always seemed to be a sort of underlying anger in her. She was ambitious, an intellectual. She felt my father limited her. She wanted so much out of life and didn't get it. You may have realized that when you talked to her."

"I know the only time she smiled was when she spoke of marrying your father. I think now her concern is you."

"She's always had her hopes for me." Tyler ran his knuckles gently over her cheek. "You know what? Last night, I dreamed *you* were pregnant."

"I should have told you. I'm taking birth control pills. When I went for my last annual checkup, I asked the doctor to give me a prescription."

"When was that?"

"In April."

"Did you know then that you'd be with me?"

"I must have. After you gave me the bucket ride."

"I knew it then, too."

They went to bed shortly after that. But once they had made love again, Katherine, relaxed and drowsy, heard Tyler get up. He turned on the light, reached for his jeans. "Won't you spend the night with me?" she asked.

"I need to meet my father at home early tomorrow morning to go to our work site."

"You'll be driving the bucket truck again?"

"No, we can't use it for this job. The tree we are taking down is back behind the client's house. It's too tight to get the truck in there."

"So how will you cut the tree?"

"We climb up into it."

"That sounds dangerous."

"We'll wear harnesses. It's okay, we've done it hundreds of times. Forget about what I'm doing. Just read my novel tomorrow. It's not that long. I'll try to get here between seven and eight again, okay?"

"Okay." Katherine pulled on a robe and followed him to the front door. There they paused and gave each other a quick kiss. But when she closed the door behind him, she remembered what his mother had said about the danger, and her eyes grew troubled.

****

She read the novel all the next day. It was about a father and son and their close relationship, a mother jealous of the relationship, the son finally growing up and leaving both parents for his own life, told from all three points of view. The style was riveting, at times poetic. Katherine made some notations, but felt it was beyond the scope of her abilities to do it justice as a critic.

Knowing the novel had to be submitted somewhere, she made an impulsive decision. She picked up her phone and tapped in a number. The phone rang, and a woman's voice said, "University of Georgia English Department."

"This is Katherine Holiday. I'm an instructor in the English Department. I was wondering if I could have an appointment with Dr. Flatt. I need to ask his advice about something."

"Oh yes, I remember you, Ms. Holiday. I'm sure you can have an appointment. Let me check Dr. Flatt's schedule. When would you like to come in?"

"As soon as possible. My schedule is flexible."

"Hmm, let's see. How about tomorrow at two o'clock?"

"That's fine. I'll be there."

"Is there anything specific I can tell Dr. Flatt about the reason for your appointment?"

"I want to confer with him about one of my former students."

"I see. All right then. We'll see you tomorrow."

That evening, as Katherine waited for Tyler to come, her phone rang. It was Tyler. "Katherine—I can't come tonight."

"Is something wrong?"

"My mother's condition has gotten worse. They're sending a hospice nurse here tomorrow."

"Oh, I'm so sorry, Tyler. Is there anything I can do?"

"Maybe you could come out here?"

"Of course," she said. "I'll leave right now."

She'd made a special dish—shrimp scampi—for their dinner. Should she bring it? She put the sauce and rice in plastic containers and put them with frozen gel packs in an ice chest. If they wanted food, she would have it. She quickly brushed her hair, decided her clothes were suitable—lightweight cargo pants and a scoop-necked red T-shirt, sandals—and went out to her car with her purse over her shoulder and the ice chest in her arms. After the half-hour drive to Farmingdale, the sun was low in the west. When she pulled into his parents' parking area, Tyler came out on the porch to meet her. He was still in his work clothes.

"I'm glad you're here," he said.

"How is she?"

"Not good. Maybe you could talk with her."

"Of course. How is your father?"

"He's been here all afternoon. He left the work site at three."

"And you stayed on?"

"The crew and I finished the job. I think my father had the harder time."

"I brought some food. Will you want it?"

"It would be good for my father to eat something."

"And for you, too."

She turned toward the car, but he said, "I'll get it."

She handed him the car keys. "It's in the ice chest in the trunk."

He picked up the chest, then followed her into the house. They had set a bed up in the living room for his mother, and Tyler motioned to Katherine to go in while he set the chest on the kitchen counter.

When she entered, his father was sitting beside the bed. His wife's eyes were closed. He rose. "Thank you for coming," he said. "The pain pills they gave me for her have put her to sleep. The hospice nurse will set up a morphine drip tomorrow."

"I brought some supper. I think you should eat."

Tyler entered then. "You go take care of the food," he said to Katherine. "And Dad, you take a break. I'll stay here."

They left the room, and Katherine prepared the scampi, heating it in the microwave, then setting the plate of food before Mr. McHenry, who lifted his fork and did proceed to eat.

She returned to the living room. "You go eat too,"

she told Tyler. "I'll stay with your mother."

He hesitated, but she said, "Go!" He reached up, squeezed her hand, and left. She seated herself beside the bed. The woman's face was pale and pinched. Each breath seemed to be an effort. Katherine could see the bony ridge of her nose, her cheekbones. *This is dying. How long will it take?*

The woman seemed then to sense her presence, for she moaned a little and opened her eyes. She turned her head and looked at Katherine.

"I'm Katherine Holiday—remember me? Tyler's friend."

"Oh, yes," said the woman. "You are me."

Katherine's lips parted in surprise. Was the woman delirious?

"You are the young me," the woman said. "And you are in love."

Perhaps, after all, the dying have insights, thought Katherine. Her eyes not leaving the woman's, she nodded.

"It's a trap," the woman said.

"A trap?"

"Love is a trap. Beware, my dear. You are me, and Tyler is my Sam, and you are in love with him. But he's different from you, and he cannot change." She smiled a little. "I had hopes for Tyler. I tried so hard with him. I homeschooled him until tenth grade, you know."

"I didn't know," said Katherine.

"He was a wonderful student. But I see it now at last. Tyler will not get a college degree. Even you cannot make him. He will keep on working with the tree service. He has become his father."

The woman's eyes closed again, and she was quiet.

Katherine thought perhaps she had gone back to sleep. Then suddenly the woman opened her eyes and spoke. "There was a saying my grandmother had, written on a tile hanging in her kitchen. It said, 'Kissin' don't last. Good cookin' do.' " She turned her face again to Katherine. "What you need to remember, my dear, is the first part."

"The first part?"

"Kissin' don't last," said the woman.

"Love lasts."

"That's what I thought, too," said the woman. "And I thought Sam would escape the path that life had laid out for him, but he did not. He didn't even want to. But his is a narrow, restricted path. It does not include the life of the mind, or adventure, or travel. So when my passion died, I had just one goal—to raise my son and help him escape. I see now I failed. I just want you to know what you'd be getting into with Tyler."

Katherine put her hand on the woman's shriveled arm. "Tyler is not narrow and restricted, Mrs. McHenry. He is very talented. He has a wonderful mind, he is skilled in his profession—and he's an amazing writer. I've just read his novel. He will be famous someday. I am sure of it."

The woman looked at Katherine for a moment, as if she did not comprehend. Then her eyes closed, and she slept again.

****

"That shrimp dish was very good, Katherine," Mr. McHenry said. "Thank you."

Tyler was in the living room with his mother. Katherine was putting dishes in the dishwasher. "I'm glad you liked it, Mr. McHenry."

"Sam," he said.

"Sam." She wiped the table and counters and hung up the dishcloth. "Will someone stay with her tonight?"

"I will," said the man. "I can sleep on the couch. Goodnight, Katherine." He kissed her cheek and went to the living room, and shortly after, Tyler came into the kitchen.

"Come with me," he said.

She followed him across the lawn to the trailer. When they entered, he led her down the hall she had seen before and pushed open a door. An unmade double bed took up almost the whole room. Tyler went to a drawer and pulled out a blue cotton T-shirt that he handed to her. "Go ahead to the bathroom. There's a new toothbrush in the medicine cabinet and towels in the closet. When you're finished, I'll take a shower."

Katherine went to the bathroom, washed her face and brushed her teeth, then returned to the bedroom. Tyler left, and she heard the shower running. She took off her clothes, folded them on a chair squeezed in the corner, and put on the T-shirt. It was way too big, but she liked its soft material and comfortable looseness. She sat on the bed and waited until Tyler came in, a towel around his hips. He sat beside her.

"My mother homeschooled me, you know. "

"She told me that today."

"Up through tenth grade she would spend hours and hours with me on her loves—literature, languages and history. She was a great teacher, and I guess I was her ideal student. I loved learning from her. She wasn't as strong in math and the sciences, but my father helped in those areas, with his on-the-job training. After tenth grade, though, I was starting to get restless, and my father agreed that I should go to the public high school for the last two years. And then I didn't go to college. I chose to work with my father." He paused. His voice became husky. "I didn't turn out the way she wanted."

Katherine put her arms around him. "You will be something *better* than what she wanted. I read your novel today. It is wonderful. I believe it will be published someday."

"Even if that happens, my mother won't know."

"I told her about your book tonight and how good it was. I told her you would be famous someday." *I just hope she understood and believed me.*

Tyler, too, seemed to have his doubts. He turned to Katherine and rested his face against her. They did not make love that night. She just held him, wishing there was more she could do.

The next morning Tyler was up before dawn, his working self again. "I need to meet the crew at the work site," he said. "Dad will stay here for the hospice nurse. I'll try to get back from work early."

Katherine, not yet fully awake, looked up from the bed. "I have to go home. I have an appointment this afternoon. Is that all right?"

He nodded.

"I'll be back by four. I can come out here again tonight and bring some supper."

"That would be great." As he started for the bedroom door, she said, "Tyler." He turned, went back to her, and kissed her goodbye.

Not much later, as it began to get light, Katherine rose and dressed. She drove to her house, ate a quick breakfast, then took Tyler's manuscript to a photocopy center. She wanted to have a copy for Dr. Flatt in case he would be willing to read it. She needed the advice of someone who would know better than she did what to do next to get the novel published.

Two o'clock found her at the English department office, as scheduled. "Hello, Ms. Holiday," Dr. Flatt's secretary said. "Go on in. He's waiting for you."

Katherine felt butterflies in her stomach as she walked to the open inner door and lightly knocked.

"Ms. Holiday, come in. I didn't expect to see you again so soon."

Katherine advanced into the room. "I need your advice about something."

"Well, sit down. What is it?"

Katherine sat. "One of the students I had last semester is, I believe, a very talented writer. He has written a novel, and I think it's publishable. But how should he proceed?"

"Ah, it's a jungle out there in the publishing world. There are many talented writers. And many, many books being published—some by traditional presses, some self-published. It's like those 'mackerel crowded seas' Yeats wrote about."

Katherine bit her lip. "I was wondering, Dr. Flatt, if you would take a look at his novel? I wouldn't expect you to read the whole thing. But maybe just the first chapter?"

"I suppose you have the novel with you in that envelope there."

"Yes."

He held out his hand with a sigh. "Let me see." Remembering her feelings about Carrie, the woman poet in her class, Katherine cringed inwardly. But she handed it to him, and he slid the pack of photocopied sheets out of the envelope. "Ah," he said, looking at the title page, "by Tyler McHenry."

"Yes," said Katherine.

"The young man in your evening composition class."

Katherine felt her cheeks warm. He had remembered the name in Gene's evaluation. "Tyler McHenry shouldn't have been in that class. He was way beyond all the other students. He never took the placement tests."

He looked at her in a speculative way.

"If you don't have time to read any of it, I understand," she said.

He shook his head. "I'll take a look."

"Tyler doesn't know I'm showing this to you. But if you think it has potential, perhaps you can give some advice about what to do with it."

He shoved the papers back into the envelope. "I will get back to you, Ms. Holiday."

"Thank you so much." She stood and somewhat shyly held out her hand.

He took it and gave her a little smile. "This is just a professional interest?"

"It's a professional interest," she said.

****

At home that afternoon, preparing fried chicken, Katherine heard her cell phone ring. She saw that it was Tyler. She answered. "Tyler?"

"She is gone."

"What?" Katherine could not process his message fully.

"My mother died around four o'clock this afternoon. Sooner than they expected."

She gripped the phone tightly. "Oh, Tyler. I am so sorry."

"She'd had the morphine drip and was resting comfortably. We were both with her." He paused. "Can you come?"

"I will be there right away."
****

Mrs. McHenry was cremated, in accordance with her wishes. The day after they were given the urn containing her ashes, Katherine sat with Tyler and his father at the kitchen table discussing what kind of memorial service to have.

"She wasn't a member of a church," said Tyler. "She believed, like Ralph Waldo Emerson, that God is in everyone. If she was asked what her religion was, she'd probably say Transcendentalist."

"She didn't really have many friends," added her husband. "She kept to herself here in this house, teaching Tyler and these past eight years watching old movies and reading, always reading. I think it might be best just for the three of us to take her ashes to Jekyll Island and scatter them in the ocean, the way she requested. That's what she wanted."

"We can have our own ceremony," said Katherine. "Tyler, you could read a passage from Emerson. And you each could say something about her, maybe describe a memory."

Tyler nodded. "We'll rent a boat. I'll get online and find one."

"Get one for a Sunday as soon as possible," Mr. McHenry said.
****

The third Sunday in June found them on the deck of

a small shrimp boat three nautical miles from the Jekyll Island shoreline, the required distance for the dispersal of ashes. The retired owner, a taciturn old man who now took tourists, fishing parties—or occasionally mourners distributing ashes—out on the water, turned off the motor and watched impassively as the boat drifted, rising and falling rhythmically on the waves. His three passengers moved to the rail.

Holding the urn, Tyler's father spoke first. "Ella Tyler, you were just out of high school when we met that summer. Do you remember? I was with my father's crew, cutting trees in the city park. You were there with your girlfriends. I saw you watching me and thought you were beautiful. When the workday was over, I went over and talked with you. We ended up going to the fairgrounds together. We ate cotton candy and hot dogs and went on the rides until it got dark—and then drove to the lake and parked in my old car almost until sunrise. That was how it started. I don't think your parents were happy about us, but you were set on marrying me, and I promised them I'd always take care of you." He paused and swallowed. "At least, I did that."

Katherine felt a little shiver. That sudden infatuation—it was like her and Tyler.

It was Tyler's turn. "Mom, you homeschooled me for eleven years. You introduced me to languages, literature, and art. You made me think about what we read. I think this passage from Emerson's 'American Scholar' suggests some of what you were trying to convey to me." He looked down at the sheet of paper in his hand. " '*There is then creative reading as well as creative writing... It is remarkable the character of the pleasure we derive from the best books... There is awe mixed with the joy of surprise when a poet who lived in some past world two or three hundred years ago says that which lies close to our own soul, which we also had thought and said...'* Our days were filled with that kind of writing and reading. What you taught in those years will always be a part of me."

He pocketed the paper. He and his father leaned over the rail and together turned the urn downward. The ashes spilled out and scattered onto the water. The three of them stood there for long moments, watching the waves bear them away. Then Tyler's father turned and nodded to the old shrimper sitting at the wheel. The motor roared to life, and the boat turned toward shore.

Chapter Seven

During the following week, Katherine thought often of his mother's ashes washing out into the ocean. It had seemed a peaceful end, yet it made her sad too. She tried to divert herself, reading novels and the local papers. The police were still calling for leads in the death of Dr. Morang, and the Psychology Department was offering a reward for information leading to the arrest of the killer. At least, Katherine thought, Tyler's mother's death was a natural one—not a sudden, violent one before her time.

Since the Jekyll Island ceremony, Katherine had not seen Tyler, and she'd talked with him by phone only briefly. He didn't seem to know when he could come to her again. All he'd said was, "Work's been crazy, and Dad and I have been going through Mom's things." On Friday evening, Katherine was reading a Faulkner novel she hadn't read before and feeling rather sorry for herself when she heard a knock on the front door. Tyler, at last!

She tossed aside the book and tried not to rush to the door. There he stood, handsome as ever, his sun-streaked hair thick, in need of a haircut. He wore his usual jeans and a work T-shirt revealing the muscular build that so moved her. He gave her one of his smiles, the creases deepening in each of his cheeks. "Hi," he said.

"Hi." But she waited a moment before unlocking and opening the screen door—to make him pay a little penance for his five-day absence. Once she let him in, he immediately closed the door and reached for her. She stepped back.

"I've had a shower this time," he said.

Katherine's heart softened like melted wax. She walked into his arms.

"I've missed you," he said, and kissed her.

"I know taking care of your mother's things has been hard," she said when he drew back.

"It's harder for Dad, but I'm glad he didn't want to put it off. He's right. It's better this way." He stopped then, looking down at her. "Shall we make up for lost time?"

She nodded, and within moments, they were indeed in the bedroom making up for lost time. Afterward they lay facing each other, content.

After a few minutes Katherine said, "I've been apartment hunting."

"Did you find anything?"

She traced her fingers over his chest. "There's one that might work. It's in a complex just down the street called White Bluffs." She paused. "If I take this apartment by myself, will you be able to visit me more often than you do now?"

"I don't want to *visit* you," said Taylor.

Her fingers stopped moving. "What do you mean?"

"Katherine." Impulsively, Tyler took her face between his hands. "Don't get an apartment by yourself. I don't like being away from you, I don't like you living alone, especially after that murder, and I know I'm not with you as much as I should be. Let's just get married. Come live with me."

Katherine was shocked. Her thoughts flashed back to when she'd spent the night in his doublewide. Lying in Tyler's arms, she had awakened. Water was dripping in the bathroom and the lights of cars on the highway flashed through the window blinds. She remembered then the words of the woman who had died in the nearby house: "Kissin' don't last...."

She drew slightly away from him. Tyler was watching her face. "You don't want to marry me?"

Katherine could not answer.

"I get it. You're a teacher with a master's degree. You want to get a doctorate. What would people think if you married someone who'd never been to college?" He threw back the sheet that was over them and reached for his jeans.

"Tyler, that is not it at all."

He pulled on the jeans, reached for his shirt.

"Tyler, please. It's just that there's a lot involved in getting married."

"There doesn't have to be."

She pulled on her robe and followed him out into the hall. "Your novel, Tyler. I wanted to talk with you tonight about your novel."

He turned to her then, hitching the jeans up on his hips.

"I told you how much I liked it. I've given a copy to Dr. Flatt, the head of the English Department. He said he'd look at it and tell us what to do."

"You gave it to someone without asking me?"

"We need someone with more experience than I have," said Katherine. "Dr. Flatt has been very good to me. I think he will help—"

"You should have asked me, Katherine!" He opened the front door and walked out with that angry stride that she remembered from the beginning of the semester when he'd realized she suspected him of plagiarism. She heard the truck door slam and the engine rev up. His red taillights moved rapidly down the driveway and on to the road.

****

Shit, he could still see it. Her look of shock, even maybe of horror, when he mentioned getting married. If they married, Katherine would be like his mother, looking down on his profession. Both of them were elitists—both thought getting a college education was the only way of life. After all, who did Katherine turn to for advice about his novel? An academic, the head of the English department, a Dr. somebody. Her feelings would come out more and more as time passed. *This whole relationship is a mistake*

Tyler swung into the parking lot of the Dark Owl Lounge. Inside, he looked around. There was Tonya at a corner table with someone. He strode over. "Hi, there."

Tonya looked up. "Tyler. I thought you were dead."

He laughed. "Disappointed?"

She smiled. "Do you know Flick? He tends bar here. He's taking a break."

Tyler held out his hand. "We've met."

Flick was a big hulking guy with greasy dark hair. He took Tyler's hand. "Tonya's right. You haven't been by in a long time."

Tyler sat down at their table. "What is it they say about absence?"

Tonya looked at him with a little pout. "I'm not sure that saying is right."

"Hey, Flick, when your break's over, tell them to get me a Bud, will you?" Tyler said.

Flick rose from the table with some effort and spoke

to Tonya. "I've gotta get back. Don't let him break your heart."

She smiled up at Flick. "Don't worry." When he left, she looked down into her drink.

"So what have you been doing? Playing Shakespeare?"

Tyler laughed and reached for her hand. "Fair enough."

"I'm serious, Tyler. I don't like this writing stuff you do. That's no way to spend your nights."

"You're probably right."

She leaned closer to him. "I can show you a better way to spend your time."

Tyler turned as the waitress brought him a bottle of beer. "Thanks." He took a long swallow.

"You want to come back to my place?"

Tyler reflected. "Okay."

"Okay, you'll come? I came here with my girlfriends. Will you give me a ride home?"

"Sure." They stood. Carrying the bottle, he passed the bar, tossed a bill on the counter, and, as Flick looked after them, escorted Tonya into the night.

****

All the next day Katherine felt almost sick about the way the evening had ended. Yet she also realized why she responded as she had when Tyler said, "Let's get married."

It was in part the impracticality of moving into his trailer. But that was not all. Although she'd known him for six months, she'd actually been with him for only one. Everything had happened so fast, accelerated perhaps by the emotion of his mother's death. Her parents hadn't even met him. What would her father think of this relationship? Would he feel as he had years ago about her prom date, Tony Brunetto? And more: her feelings for Tyler were strong, but could they be, as his mother had said, only infatuation? Their marriage might end up being an unhappy one between two very different people, like his parents' marriage.

Then she wondered if she had been wrong to give a copy of the manuscript to Dr. Flatt without asking Tyler. It had seemed the next step in deciding what to do to publish his book. Why should he be angry? Maybe that was an indication of problems they might have in the future.

That evening she sat on her front porch, hoping Tyler would call or that his truck might pull into her driveway. She knew he'd probably worked all day, but Saturday night should be theirs. Finally, she picked up her phone and tapped in his number. The call went to voice mail. "Please leave a message after the beep," the taut female voice directed her. The leave-a-message beep came, but she could not think what to say. She pressed the disconnect button.

Dog tags jangled on the street on front of her house and a male voice said, "No, boy!" A dog was trying to run up into her yard. She saw that the voice belonged to Henry Armstid, her lawyer neighbor, who was standing on the sidewalk and pulling back on the leash of a small collie. He looked up and saw her. "Hi, Katherine."

"Henry! Have you gotten a dog?"

"I just got him. He's a rescue. His name is Shelby."

"He is beautiful." Katherine could not resist going down to the sidewalk. "Will he let me pet him?"

"I think so. He seems friendly around people."

Katherine held out her hand, palm up, for Shelby to

sniff, and when he seemed satisfied, patted his head.

"You'll have to let me know if he barks and bothers you when I have him out in the yard," Henry said. "Your house is so close to mine."

"Actually, I'll be moving in a month. Professor Foster and his wife are coming back to Athens at the beginning of August. My housesitting days will be over."

Henry looked at her in a warm way through his horn-rimmed glasses. "I'm sorry to hear you're leaving. It's been nice having you in the neighborhood, even if I haven't seen as much of you as I'd have liked. Hey, have you had dinner?"

"No."

"There's a new restaurant on Baxter Street, Fresh Farm. I was thinking of going there to eat sometime. Want to come there with me tonight?"

"I don't know. I may have a friend stopping by. Let me check my phone messages." Katherine pulled it out of her pocket. *Nothing*. "No, I guess he's not," she said.

"So how about it?"

If Tyler is mad at me and staying away, I am not going to sit around the house all evening. "All right. That sounds nice. I'll just get my purse and lock up."

"I'll bring Shelby home and stop for you in just a minute." While she waited on the porch for Henry's Mercedes to come by, Katherine turned off her phone.

****

The food had been good, the conversation friendly. Henry told her about his work at his law firm, and she told him about her teaching. As they walked to his car after dinner, Henry asked, "Want to go get a drink or something?"

"I think I'd better get home."

"Oh, come on," Henry said.

"I really can't go out for a drink tonight."

"You're thinking your friend might still come by?"

"Something like that."

"Maybe another time then?"

"Maybe."

Henry drove to her house and pulled up to the curb in front. A truck was parked in her driveway. On its door was painted *McHenry's Tree Service*. A dark figure sat in a rocker on her porch. She'd forgotten to turn on the porch light.

"Your friend?" asked Henry.

"Yes," said Katherine. She turned and smiled apologetically at Henry. "Thank you so much for dinner."

"Any time," said Henry.

Katherine got out of the car and went up the walk to the porch, pausing at the bottom step. She heard Henry's car idling by the curb as if he were watching to be sure she was all right. Perhaps he was remembering the murder on campus, the murder which had never been solved.

The dark figure that was Tyler stood up. She and he looked at each other for a moment. Then Katherine went up the steps to him, put her arms around his waist, and leaned against him. His arms closed around her. She heard Henry's car leave the curb and move on down the street.

"I'm sorry." Katherine's words were muffled against Tyler's chest.

He leaned down to kiss her hair. "So am I."

They held each other for long moments. Then Katherine stepped away as if in slow motion and unlocked the door. He followed her inside. They went to the room the Fosters called the library, with its floor-to-ceiling bookcases filled with books and artifacts, and sat on the couch.

"I should have asked you if I could give Dr. Flatt a copy of your novel."

"I overreacted. Many people besides you and me will have to read it if it's going to be published. I'll have to get used to it." Tyler paused. "I shouldn't have asked you to marry me just out of the blue. It was a sudden, crazy impulse."

"I shouldn't have reacted the way I did." She touched his cheek. "I've never felt about anyone the way I feel about you."

"And I've never felt about anyone the way I feel about you." They sat silent. Then he said, "I have a confession to make. I was so mad last night I...I picked up an old girlfriend. I went back to her place."

Shocked, Katherine pulled away from him. "After you'd just been with me?"

He bowed his head. "Then I couldn't do it. I couldn't stay with her. I just left."

"Oh, Tyler." She looked at him. "I went out to dinner with someone tonight—you saw him drop me off. It was the same."

He lifted her hand and kissed it. "Someday, in case we ever do feel it's right for us to get married, do you want me to ask you in one of the ways you read about? A diamond ring in a box of chocolates? A flashing sign on the screen at a football game? Should I kneel?"

Laughing, Katherine shook her head. "Just ask."

He leaned forward then, and they kissed. A warm liquid sense of relief spread through Katherine. Feeling his body against hers, the warmth turned to the heat of desire. There came to her a vision of herself standing next to Tyler—in a church, in a courthouse, or somewhere, the place didn't matter—reciting the wedding vows: "for better or worse, in sickness and in health, for richer and poorer..." The vision was breathtaking in its vividness.

She would try to forget the warnings of Tyler's mother with her flashing flint-colored eyes.

****

On a Saturday in July Katherine met Marian and Christy for lunch at the Hilltop Restaurant. Marian spoke right away. "We haven't heard from you in a long time, and you haven't posted on Facebook. What has happened with your sexy student? Are you seeing him?"

"Yes," said Katherine.

"And?"

"I think it's really serious."

"How serious?" asked Marian. "Like live-with-him serious? Marriage serious?" The two girls leaned forward on the table.

"Maybe."

Christy regarded her closely. "You've always dated college guys, grad students like Robert Mason, once even a professor."

"Tyler is better than any of them."

"Then when can we meet him?" asked Marian.

"I don't know. But I want you to."

Christy spoke thoughtfully. "Maybe we should all have a tailgate once football season starts."

"Let's do that!" exclaimed Katherine. Surely once they met Tyler, they would see why she had fallen in love.

****

On Monday morning, Katherine's phone buzzed. She tapped the connect button. "Hello."

"Ms. Holiday, Bill Flatt here. I've read your student's novel."

Her pulse quickened. "You have?"

"I think you should bring him in to talk to me. I'd like to meet him, and I have some ideas to run by him. When could you come?"

"Tyler works every weekday, but I'm sure he could take some time off for this."

"How about tomorrow? I'll be here in my office all afternoon and have no appointments. Just come by whenever he can."

"I'll check with Tyler, but I think that will work."

"Fine. Call me if there's a problem." Dr. Flatt rang off.

Excited, she called Tyler, knowing he must be up in a tree somewhere, but she could leave him a message. This time she knew what to say.

On Tuesday afternoon she drove Tyler to the campus and parked her car in the lot assigned to her. They walked the three blocks to Park Hall and entered its cool interior. Not many students were around in the summer, and the few classes offered were held in the morning. Katherine led Tyler up the stairs to the English Department office.

"Hello, Ms. Holiday," the secretary greeted her. Her eyes moved to Tyler and widened. He was freshly showered and dressed not in work clothes, though casually—in jeans and his white Oxford shirt, open at the neck.

"This is Tyler McHenry," Katherine said. "Dr. Flatt

is expecting us."

The secretary came back to attention. "Yes." She rose and walked over to Dr. Flatt's office door. "Ms. Holiday and Mr. McHenry are here."

Dr. Flatt came to the office door. He motioned to them. "Come on in." Once they were in the office, he held out his hand to Katherine. Taking it, she said, "Dr. Flatt, this is Tyler McHenry."

"Ah," said Dr. Flatt, looking Tyler up and down as they shook hands. "I'm glad to meet you. Come in, sit down."

Dr. Flatt sat in his large office chair as Katherine and Tyler took the two chairs on the opposite side of his desk. He picked up the manuscript of Tyler's novel, which had been lying there. "I read the whole thing. This, young man, is very impressive."

Tyler looked up in surprise. His eyes began to shine. "Thank you, sir." There was a tremor of excitement in his voice.

"I lent the manuscript to Dr. Carmella Hogan, the head of our creative writing department. She also read it and was impressed as well. She gave me a list of agents for you to contact and suggested you describe it as a *Bildungsroman*, a coming-of-age novel. She says to use her name when you write to them. Dr. Hogan is quite well-known, so that should get their attention. This list should save you a good deal of time." He held out a sheet of paper.

Tyler reached out and took it with care. He cleared his throat, and Katherine knew he was trying to make his voice sound normal when he said again, "Thank you."

"I'm sure at least one of these agents will be interested in seeing a sample of your novel," went on Dr.

Flatt. "And in representing you once they read the whole thing."

"And then the agent will find Tyler a publisher?" asked Katherine.

"Once he or she takes you on, that's the agent's job—to get you the best possible publisher and deal," said Dr. Flatt. "I'm not in the field of fiction publishing, but I think you may do very well with this novel, son. And so does Dr. Hogan." Dr. Flatt slid the manuscript back into its manila envelope and handed it to Tyler. "Google the agents on Dr. Hogan's list for their addresses and contact them as soon as you can."

"I will."

"It appears you've had a good advocate in Ms. Holiday."

"Yes, sir, a very good advocate."

"It's most unusual to find someone like you in a first-year composition course. I can see why Ms. Holiday has taken a special interest in you, both professionally and...personally. What is your educational background?"

"My mother homeschooled me through tenth grade. She gave me a much more advanced curriculum in the humanities than I'd have gotten in the public—or even the private—schools. As a junior, I started going to the public high school. There, I found myself focusing on the things she hadn't been able to give me—team sports, social life. I'd also been working with my father's tree service through the years. He'd inherited it from his father, and after I graduated from high school, it just seemed natural that I continue working there. Now I co-own the business with my father."

"But you've started working on a college degree?"

"My mother had always wanted me to go to college, had tried to talk me into it for years. Last year she became terminally ill, so I finally took a course. It was for her. She passed away a few weeks ago."

"Ah, I'm sorry." Dr. Flatt paused. "Well, whatever you decide to do about college now, son, I think you have a real talent in writing. Maybe it's more original since you haven't been shaped by creative writing courses." He smiled a little. "Faulkner never took any either." He stood then and came around his desk. "You two keep me informed about the novel. Oh—and Katherine, I want you to teach that adult composition class after all next fall. That is, if you'd still like to."

"Oh, yes," said Katherine. "I would. Thank you, Dr. Flatt."

"I'm sorry that evaluation raised a question about your...about you. I think whoever wrote it misunderstood the situation. And I was wrong to reassign your evening class based just on that one evaluation. I was too hasty, still thinking about that campus murder I guess. I apologize." He turned to Tyler. "I think you have a good future ahead, Mr. McHenry. I'm glad to have met you."

"I'm glad to have met you, sir. Thank you again—for everything." They shook hands again all around, and Dr. Flatt escorted them to his office door. Outside in the cool dim corridor, walking toward the exit door, Tyler and Katherine clasped hands in silent celebration.

On the way home she said, "Did you notice—it didn't seem to matter to Dr. Flatt at all that you don't have a college degree."

"I guess he saw I have a really unusual background." Tyler paused. "But I have something to ask you. What was Dr. Flatt talking about when he said he was *reassigning* you to the adult composition class in the fall? Had he taken it away from you?"

"He—he thought he might have to give me only day classes," said Katherine.

"What was the evaluation he mentioned?"

"Oh, did he mention an evaluation?"

"You know he did, Katherine. Tell me."

"I'm not sure what he meant." She turned into her driveway and turned off the ignition.

"Did that shit Gene say something about us in his evaluation of your class?"

She looked away, reaching for the door handle.

"Look at me, Katherine."

Reluctantly she turned and met his eyes. He saw the answer there. "That bastard!" Tyler hit the dashboard of her car with his fist.

"Tyler, it's all over now. And we don't know for sure who…"

"Yes, we do," said Tyler.

She leaned over to him, though at first he tried to avoid her, and put her hand on his cheek. "Don't let anything spoil this time for us. Let's go in and have a drink to celebrate what Dr. Flatt said about your novel."

****

Tyler knew, that night after he'd tried to stay with Tonya, that Katherine had taken his desire for anyone else. It was even clearer as she became his partner in sending out inquiry letters to agents about his novel. But he also came to realize that he was not set up for the marriage he'd so impulsively suggested—not when he lived in his dingy doublewide. She was used to better, and hell, it didn't used to matter, but he always knew someday he'd want a better place too. In fact, he'd fantasized about the kind of place he wanted to own someday.

There was a property he'd recently seen while doing some work for a client—in a beautiful wooded area near the town. He remembered a conversation with the owner after his day of work there. "I'm going to put this up for sale soon. That's why I wanted those trees trimmed. You did a great job, Mr. McHenry. Thanks."

Tyler hadn't thought much about it at the time, but now images of that rustic cottage came back to him. He pulled out his phone, looked up the client, and tapped on his name.

****

Over the rest of the week Katherine printed out the website material on the ten agents on Dr. Flatt's list, and she and Tyler spent the next Friday evening studying it. Most of the agents wanted a letter of inquiry, a synopsis, and the first five, ten, or twenty pages of the manuscript. She and Tyler finally decided, based on the agents' descriptions, which ones would be most interested in his novel. Then together they drafted a synopsis and letters of inquiry to each of five agents.

"Send me your novel as an attachment and I'll send out whatever number of pages they want and your other materials," said Katherine.

"I should be doing that myself," said Tyler.

"You're busy working, and I have time this summer. I want to do it. We can set up a special email account for this and have it on both my computer and yours."

"All right," said Tyler. "But you have to promise me something. I'm not working tomorrow and I want to take you somewhere in the morning early, before it gets too hot. Will you go with me?"

"Where is 'somewhere'?"

"It's a surprise."

"So you'll spend the whole night with me tonight?" Katherine felt that was surprise enough.

Saturday morning dawned bright and pleasant for a Georgia July. At seven o'clock, they left in Tyler's truck. "This place I'm taking you to will be beautiful this morning," he said.

"You're building suspense."

He smiled. She loved his smile—his blue eyes bright, his lower lip a little larger than his upper, his mischievous, happy look. She looked out at the road he was taking. "It looks like we're going to Oconee Forest."

"It's a few miles beyond that." Tyler passed the entrance to Oconee Forest, and before long turned onto a private dirt road that curved through a shady wood. Ferns lined the side of the road.

"What is this?"

"You'll see in a minute." Tyler turned into a driveway and stopped in a pebbled parking area. "Come on," he said. They got out of the car, and he led her down a path to a brown-stained shingled rustic cottage with a screened porch across the front. "This is what I want to show you."

Katherine followed Tyler to the locked porch door. He produced a key, unlocked it, and pushed it open. The porch looked unused and a bit dusty with plant pollen that had blown through the screens, but even like this, it was inviting. There was a wooden table and chairs for eating, a porch swing, and the bare frames of lounge chairs that would take cushions. Tyler went to the interior door and unlocked it. She followed him inside.

They entered a kitchen—with double sink, full-sized refrigerator, and gas stove. They continued walking through the house. Down a little hall from the kitchen was a laundry room, and a bathroom with a shower and tub. Farther down the hall, a door opened into a large master bedroom. On the other side of the kitchen was a dining area with glass doors that looked out into the woods. And off the dining area was a living room with couch, chairs, and a stone fireplace. Braided rugs were on the floor. The walls were of knotty pine. There were stairs against one of the living room walls.

"Come upstairs," said Tyler. At the top was another hall. Tyler opened the doors along it to reveal three more furnished bedrooms and another full bath.

"This cottage is much larger than it looks from outside!" she exclaimed.

"It has central air and heat, and its own well for the water supply. Two acres of land come with it. Follow the dirt road for another half mile, and you come to a lake with a little beach for residents of this area to use."

"How did you find this?"

"One of our clients had this property and came here weekends as a sort of escape from town. But now he's bought a place in Highlands, North Carolina, so he wants sell this. I checked with him this week—he was just about to put it on the market. I told him I was interested."

"Can you afford it?"

"Katherine, my life's been simple. I didn't buy fancy clothes and cars. I've lived rent-free in that trailer. But I'm part owner of a successful business. So I've saved some money, and I realize I should spend it for something important. I've always wanted a place like this, in the woods. Yes, I can afford it." He paused. "This is not far from town and the University. It would work for you too."

"One of these bedrooms up here could be your office, where you can write."

"And another one could be yours, for your teaching—and your studies if you do go on for a PhD. A lot of the furniture is included, though I know we'd change some of it."

"Oh, Tyler!"

He gave her a pleased smile. "So you like it?"

"I love it!"

"Then don't worry about finding an apartment by August first. I'll make an offer on this. I'm sure the owner and I will come to an agreement, and you can move in here with me."

Katherine hugged him joyfully. But she noticed he did not mention marriage again.

Chapter Eight

Katherine soon received an email from Mrs. Foster reporting that she and her husband would return on the sixth of August. With only three weeks left before she was to leave the Fosters' house, Katherine sent Tyler's materials to the agents they'd chosen, then finished updating her teaching materials. Once Tyler completed the legalities of buying the cottage in the woods at the end of July, Katherine began moving her personal things there.

Mrs. Foster asked Katherine to pick her and her husband up at the shuttle office on the day they were to return. And so on August sixth, Katherine was waiting. Right on schedule the van pulled up, and Dr. and Mrs. Foster—a short, rotund, balding man and his sandy-haired, equally rotund wife—got out, both full of smiles when they spotted her.

"Oh, my dear, it is good to see you again," said Mrs. Foster, giving her a hug.

"I know you've had a wonderful year," Katherine replied, hugging the woman in return and then her husband.

"Yes, but it will be good to be home," said Dr. Foster. They were eager, when Katherine got them to the house and their luggage was unloaded, to greet their cats and look over the gardens and the house itself.

"Everything looks perfect," Mrs. Foster said. "Our place was obviously in good hands but I have to admit, when I read about that murder on campus, I began to worry about you living here so close to campus by yourself."

"It was fine. I locked those dead bolt locks every night and felt completely safe. I've enjoyed living here. I'll just hand you my keys, and the house is yours again. I've moved my things out."

"Where will you be living now?" asked Dr. Foster.

"I have a friend who's just bought a house out past Oconee Forest. I'll be living there."

"Who is the friend?" asked the alert Mrs. Foster. "A boyfriend, perhaps?"

Katherine hesitated, then said, "Yes."

"Someone with the University?"

"No, he's an arborist. He owns a tree service with his father, and he's a writer."

"Ah, an interesting combination," said Dr. Foster.

"Their service cut down the huge magnolia across the street," said Katherine. "It was diseased and dangerous."

"I saw it was gone. That stump is huge. It must have been a big job," said Dr. Foster.

Mrs. Foster impulsively took Katherine's hand. "We're going to have a homecoming party soon. We'll invite you and your arborist friend. You'll know many people we're inviting—we are asking several English faculty members."

"I'll look forward to that."

After the Fosters hugged Katherine one last time, she went to her car. Backing out of the driveway, she looked at the house she had lived in for the past year, and where, for the past few weeks, she had created so many memories with Tyler. Although she was about to move into a new home and a new chapter in her life, this one would always hold a special place in her heart.

****

Katherine and Tyler worked hard fixing up the cottage. They scrubbed and cleaned, washed the windows, set up bookcases, put cushions on the porch chairs. It was becoming their own.

When they went to the Fosters' homecoming party, Katherine was proud to introduce Tyler. Dr. Flatt and his wife were among the guests there, as was Carmella Hogan, the silver-haired head of the creative writing department. "I am so glad to meet you," the woman told Tyler warmly, shaking his hand. "What have you heard about your novel?"

"We wrote to five of the agents you recommended," said Tyler. "We've heard from two. They said the book didn't meet their needs at this time."

"That kind of answer is hardly surprising," said Dr. Flatt, who was standing with them. "I think agents are pretty overwhelmed with queries. Also, they know what they want to sell no matter how good the book is. The percentage of rejections is high. But all you need is one affirmative."

"He's right," said Dr. Hogan. "You hear stories of people sending off manuscripts to agents and getting hundreds of rejections—then finally one takes it, sells the book to a Big Five publisher, and it becomes a bestseller. But I do think one of the agents I listed for you will be interested in your book."

"I'll try to remember that," said Tyler. "I really appreciate your help."

Katherine heard voices from across the room and turned to see Spenser Johns holding forth in his usual pompous manner to a group of young professors. His speechifying paused, and he turned toward her. His eyes flitted to Tyler, standing close at her side. He nodded his head to her in acknowledgement—then coldly, and with a rather cynical smile, turned back to his group.

Not long after that event, Christy and her husband Tom and Marian and her boyfriend Wilson invited Tyler and Katherine to a tailgate for the home football game on September twelfth with South Carolina. It could not have turned out better. Tyler fit right in, laughing and talking with them as they ate snacks, grilled hamburgers, and drank beer outside the pop-up tent Wilson had set up.

At six o'clock when it was near the time to head to the stadium for the seven o'clock game and Marian was packing up the food, Christy pulled Katherine aside. "I see what you mean about Tyler," she said. "I would never have thought it, but you and he are perfect together. And—Katherine?"

"Yes?"

"Don't tell Tom I said this, but you're right. Tyler is very sexy!"

Georgia won the game, forty-one to thirty-seven.

****

The fall semester, of course, brought not only faculty parties and football games, but classes. Katherine was busy teaching her three morning classes and the adult class at night. They were all going well, but she soon realized there was an uncomfortable situation in the evenings. Walking down the corridor of the Georgia Center for Continuing Education to her adult class shortly after the beginning of the semester, she saw Gene in a group of students. He must be taking another class, she thought, ducking quickly into her own classroom. On the next several evenings at the Center, she either did not see him or saw him only at a distance. But those few times, she thought he was looking at her.

One night as she walked into the parking lot after class, she found him leaning against the driver's side of her car, arms folded. "Ms. Holiday," he said, as she walked up. "I just thought I'd say hello. You were one of my favorite teachers."

Katherine felt uneasy in the dusk, with people who passed paying no attention to such encounters, just hurrying to their cars to get home. "You could have gotten me in real trouble with your evaluation."

"I just told the truth....You know, now you could go out with *me*."

Katherine clicked her car key to unlock the door. "Please move," she said. "I need to get home."

"We could have a good time at Harry's tonight."

She moved closer to her car door, determined to get in. He stayed in position, only at the last moment moving aside and then opening it for her. After she was behind the wheel, he continued to hold the door handle. "You never read the poem I gave you," he said. " 'Killing Me Sweetly.' "

"I've had to make it a policy not to read student writing outside of class."

"Will you read it now? I think you'll find it interesting."

Katherine reached out to shut the car door. "I'm not a good poetry critic."

He continued to hold it. "Are you sure you don't you want to let down your hair and go dancing with me?"

When her only response was to start the car engine, Gene smiled unpleasantly. "I guess not. I guess you prefer the redneck type. All right. Maybe you'll change your mind about that, though. Good night, Ms. Holiday." He slammed the door—rather hard.

Katherine drove home, her lips tightly pressed together. *I shouldn't be afraid of Gene. He's just jealous of Tyler because Tyler was so outstanding in the classroom...and because I went with him to Harry's.*

Of course, he didn't know they were now in a serious relationship. She would not mention this encounter to Tyler, nor would she mention Tyler to Gene, afraid, after that restroom fight, of what might happen. She would just stay away from him at the Center as best she could and hope not to see him again in the parking lot. The paranoia on campus since Dr. Morang's murder had faded along with the publicity. This former student was a nuisance, nothing more—but a nuisance she wished to avoid.

As the weeks went by, and there were no more sightings of Gene Whittaker, her plan seemed to work.

****

Katherine had put off telling her parents about her relationship with Tyler, but after she sent them her new physical mailing address, they'd begun asking questions about her roommates. She had answered only vaguely and changed the subject. The thought crossed her mind that she could say she was house-sitting again. She thought again of that incident in high school when her father so disapproved of her going to the prom with the high school football star....Yes, it might be hard to tell them about Tyler, who, at twenty-six without a college degree and his job so physical, might seem at first the kind of "jock" her father had deprecated. But soon she knew it was time to tell them, to make them understand and appreciate him.

When her parents next called and again asked about her new address, she took a deep breath and began, "I am living with a friend—"

Her mother interrupted. "You found a new roommate?"

"He's someone I've been dating. His name is Tyler McHenry,"

"Oh, my goodness, this is a surprise," her mother exclaimed. "Tell us about him."

This was it. "He was one of my students—"

"You're dating someone who was in one of your classes?" her father burst in. "Don't you teach only freshmen and sophomores?"

"He was in my evening class for non-traditional students, Dad. He's twenty-six. We didn't date until the class was over. He owns a business. Well, he co-owns it. With his father."

"What kind of business?"

"A tree service. He's an arborist. And he writes," she added hastily. "He has written a novel."

"Is it published?"

"Not yet. But I've read it and so have the head of the English department and the head of creative writing and they like it. He's sending it off to agents. I'm sure it's just a matter of time until it's published."

There was a silence at the other end of the line.

Katherine started speaking again. "He has an unusual background. His mother homeschooled him through tenth grade. Tyler knows more than most college graduates about literature and history. Being placed in my class was a mistake. He should have been in the honors program."

"Is he going on for a degree now?" her father asked.

"I don't know. He works full time." She paused. "Tyler may not sound like the type of person you'd expect me to be involved with, but…I think this is serious."

"How serious?"

She hesitated a moment. "Very."

Now her mother spoke. "I trust your judgement, dear, and I'm sure your father does, too. Send a picture. Let us talk to him on the phone."

"Why don't you both come down and visit us?"

They demurred at the time, but as the semester went on, Katherine continued to tell them about Tyler, in emails and phone calls, until, in mid-October they called her, ready to meet this young man. A date for a visit was set: they'd fly to Atlanta the last weekend of the month. That weekend began UGA's fall break, and most of the students would be away at Jacksonville for the Florida-Georgia football game.

Katherine worried about their visit. One evening as the date neared, she approached Tyler. "Shall my parents stay with us or shall we get them a motel?"

"They know we're living together, don't they?"

"Yes. It's just…I feel a little strange about it."

"I could sleep on the cot in my office."

"No, you're right, they know. We'll sleep in our bedroom, and they can sleep in the spare bedroom upstairs." She thought for a moment. "And we must ask your father over to meet them."

"Good idea," said Tyler. He looked at Katherine's still furrowed brow. "Everything will be fine, honey.

We've hired some new crew members so I can take time off. I'll take your car and pick up your parents at the Atlanta airport. That way they won't have to rent a car or take the shuttle to Athens."

"Shouldn't I go too?"

"Maybe it would be better for just me to go, so we can get to know each other. You know, like for a job interview." He glanced over at her and grinned. "I'll win them over. Besides," he added, "that will give you time to get things in order here and finish grading your morning class papers for Monday."

"All right," said Katherine, "but you need a haircut before they come. I can cut it."

She put a sheet around his neck and got out the kitchen shears. Soon clippings of his gold-streaked hair were lying around him on the kitchen floor. "Here, see what you think." She handed him a mirror.

"The important thing is what they will think, isn't it?" said Tyler, looking in the mirror a bit skeptically.

"Well, I think you look wonderful." Katherine looked down at him, at the white of his skin on his neck where she'd clipped up his almost shoulder-length hair, and she couldn't resist leaning down to kiss him there.

"Hey, what are you doing?" Tyler turned, grabbed her, and pulled her around to his lap.

"That was the final part of my service."

"No, there is something else needed," said Tyler, pulling off the sheet. "In the bedroom down the hall."

****

Tyler did not feel as confident as he had acted with Katherine. But under his mother's tutelage he had read many American novels. And he had prepared for her parents' visit by re-reading a couple of his survey texts of American literature and her father's book on Melville, though he hadn't told Katherine that. Now he dressed carefully in khakis, a blue button-down shirt, and his navy-blue zip-up jacket—not his work clothes, but not too formal either.

"You look great," Katherine told him, standing there, her arms folded, watching him put his wallet in his pocket and pick up her car keys. "They'll be impressed."

"So clothes make the man?" he asked, his smile a little restrained as he walked toward her.

She smoothed his shirt collar and kissed him. "They'll be impressed with *you.*"

He headed for the door. "We'll see if you're right. We should be back here in about four hours."

Soon after, he was turning onto the highway to Atlanta. *What was I thinking? I'll be spending two hours alone with Katherine's parents, meeting them for the first time…her father an academic who would surely be wary of someone like me for his daughter.* He was still asking himself that question as he stood by the large luggage carousel in the Atlanta airport, where suitcases from the flight were already tumbling down the chute. He had seen photographs of her parents, and he now scanned the incoming passengers.

There they were, a tall, bespectacled, gray-haired man, now a little stooped, in a black overcoat, holding the arm of a petite blonde woman who was eagerly looking over at the crowd already gathered at the carousel. Even as Tyler spotted them, she smiled and waved, and then spoke to her husband, who looked in Tyler's direction. They had seen his picture too.

"You must be Tyler," the woman said warmly as she approached, holding out her hand. "I'm Elizabeth

Holiday, Katherine's mother, and this is her father, Ron."

"Ron Holiday," said the man, extending his hand and regarding Tyler with what seemed a kind of reservation.

Tyler made himself smile. "Glad to meet you at last, Dr. Holiday, Mrs. Holiday. Katherine's told me so much about you." He turned to the carousel. "Do you see your luggage?"

The pair moved closer and pointed out two tweed suitcases now moving toward them. Tyler moved to grab one while Mr. Holiday retrieved the other.

"I'm parked just across the road," said Tyler. "I can get these." He was glad Katherine's father let him pull both suitcases, a little deference perhaps to his younger strength. As Tyler opened the trunk and stowed the suitcases, Mrs. Holiday turned to her husband. "Ron, you sit in front with Tyler. Your legs are so much longer than mine."

When they were all settled in the car and driving from the airport, Tyler said, "You've visited Katherine here in Athens before, haven't you?"

Her mother leaned forward in the back seat. "Yes, when she was a graduate student. Her roommates, Christy and Marian, were so nice. Do you know them?"

"Yes, we've tailgated with them. They're great."

Glancing in the rear-view mirror, Tyler saw her smile. "Katherine told me about that tailgate. She said you all had such a good time together."

Beside him, Dr. Holiday cleared his throat. "Katherine tells us you've written a novel."

"I've written it and sent sample pages to five agents. Dr. Flatt, the head of the English Department, liked it, and Dr. Carmella Hogan of creative writing gave me the names of the agents."

"Well, that's a start."

After a moment Tyler said, "I read your book on Herman Melville, sir. I was interested in how you showed his earlier potboilers, as he called them, led to plot and themes in *Moby Dick*."

"You read my book?" Dr. Holiday sounded surprised, pleased.

"His *Pierre*, too, published the next year, picks up those *Moby Dick* themes, but I didn't find it as good, actually, as the potboilers."

"*Pierre* is a pretty terrible novel, but so American—with the dark-haired and blonde heroines. Just waiting for Leslie Fiedler to write about them."

Tyler laughed, remembering his mother talking about Fiedler's *Love and Death in the American Novel*. "Ah, yes, those monsters of virtue or—well, at one point Fiedler called it 'bitchery.' "

"But I don't believe the characters in European novels are necessarily more sexually mature than those in American lit. Look at *Madame Bovary*...Emma Bovary was an immature, selfish bitch *disguising herself* for a time, at least, as the paragon of virtue."

Tyler turned on to Interstate Eighty-five and accelerated. "Emma's idea of love was certainly adolescent," he said. "But it was not Flaubert's."

By evening when Tyler, returning from the airport, pulled into the cottage parking area and he and her parents got out of the car, Katherine could tell right away that everything was all right. They were talking and laughing together as they got the luggage out of the trunk. When she ran to them, her mother hugged her and said, "Tyler is wonderful."

"He's a fine young man," her father whispered, as he, too, hugged her.

Katherine exchanged glances with Tyler, whose blue eyes were bright, his smile satisfied. Yes, she thought, he had won them over. They wouldn't mind that he didn't have a college degree—or about the sleeping arrangements.

"Come in and have a drink before dinner," she said.

****

On Saturday they took her parents on a tour of Athens and the campus, and that night Tyler's father arrived at the cottage for dinner. Katherine hugged him affectionately and introduced him to her parents. He looked handsome too, and she thought he was limping less. Tyler had told her he was throwing himself back into work since the death of his wife, organizing the jobs and hiring more crew members so they did not have to work such long hours. Over drinks before dinner, they talked about the upcoming elections, college football in general, and the reasons for Georgia's loss to Florida in the afternoon's game.

Then the conversation became more personal. Katherine's father said to Mr. McHenry, "Tyler tells me you and he are business partners."

Mr. McHenry reached over and squeezed his son's shoulder. "Yes. He's my best worker—and best friend."

"How nice you have such a relationship," said Katherine's mother. "I was sorry to hear about your wife's death."

"Call me Sam," aid Tyler's father. "Thank you." He looked as if he would say more, but decided not to.

Katherine spoke up. "I told you, Mom and Dad— Tyler's mother homeschooled him through tenth grade.

I got to meet her just before she died."

"And she scared you, didn't she?" said Tyler.

Surprised, Katherine looked at him. "A little."

There was a moment of silence, until Katherine's father said, "Ah, mothers can be scary sometimes. They are so protective of their young."

"I'm not scary to you, am I, Katherine?" asked her mother.

Katherine laughed. "Not since I was five and you spanked me for running away at the lake to try to ride the horses at Close's farm."

"And got yourself in the pasture with all those loose horses—not knowing anything about them," said her mother.

Katherine's father looked around at them all. "My wife got in the pasture with Katherine and dragged her out through the gate just as they all started galloping toward her. That's when the spanking occurred. I believe that story proves my point about mothers protecting their young."

Sam spoke up then. "I think, in our case, I was what Tyler's mother was trying to protect him from. She and I had very different views of what Tyler should be and do with his life. Many mornings, from the time he was a little tyke, I took him with me to my work sites. I began training him in my profession as soon as he was old enough to help. On the mornings he wasn't with me and most afternoons, she had him in her study room where she homeschooled him, filling his head with what she called the humanities. I guess he was always being torn between us."

Impulsively, Katherine touched the man's hand. "You and his mother may each have given Tyler a different type of education, but I think the best of both of you is in him."

****

On Sunday morning Tyler put Katherine's parents' suitcases in the trunk of her car as Katherine sat at the kitchen table doing a quick check of email on her phone.

"Katherine, come on!" Tyler called to her. "They have a plane to catch."

"Just a minute!" Hardly believing the message she had just read, Katherine jumped up and ran outside. Reaching Tyler, she held up the phone for him to see. "Tyler! An agent wants to see your book!"

"What?" He took her wrist and looked at the little screen.

"I just saw this email. The agent named Kitty Harding says she really likes the excerpt you've sent and wants to see the full manuscript!" She threw her arms about him. "Isn't that wonderful?"

"Congratulations!" exclaimed Katherine's mother, who was standing nearby.

"Great!" said her father. Katherine's parents came over and hugged Tyler too.

"Katherine said you would be famous someday," her mother said.

"I think that's a little premature," said Tyler. But he stepped back from them and looked down at the phone screen again as if to confirm what he had seen. Then he looked at Katherine, and she at him. They did not need words to express the joy they were feeling. The mood of jubilation among the four of them lasted all the way to Hartsfield airport. It was the perfect way to end the visit.

Chapter Nine

As Katherine walked down the hall to her classroom the following Tuesday, Gene Whittaker's slim dark figure separated himself from a group of students outside the next classroom and slunk up beside her. "You haven't changed your mind?"

Annoyed that he was still pestering her just when things in her life had had otherwise been going so well, she tried simply to move on by.

He blocked her way. "About going to Harry's?"

"No, I haven't changed my mind." She went into her classroom—Classroom Six again—a sanctuary where several of the students were already in their seats.

When class was over at eight-fifteen, she dreaded the walk back to her car alone in the dark in case Gene was still around. Kirk Harris, a tall, solid African American man who sat in the front row, was the last student to leave the room. "Kirk," she said, putting her final papers in her brief case. "Would you mind walking with me to my car? It—it was sounding a little strange this afternoon, and I want to be sure it starts."

"Sure, Ms. Holiday. My car is parked there, too."

She felt good with his bulk beside her as they walked to the parking lot, and he stood there as she got into her car and turned on the ignition. The car started up with a healthy growl. She rolled down her window and smiled at him.

"It sounds good, Ms. Holiday," Kirk said.

"Yes, it does. Maybe this afternoon was my imagination. Thank you, Kirk." He gave a wave, and she rolled up her window and backed out of the space.

Driving down College Station Road and on toward the cottage, with classical music playing on her radio, Katherine felt happy again. Gene had disappeared after class; hopefully he'd gotten the message. Everything was going well for her and Tyler. An agent had asked for his book, her parents loved him, his father was doing well, and the cottage was perfect for them. Now if Tyler could just forgive her for refusing to marry him when he'd suggested it…

Perhaps, though, he'd now decided they should just live together, as so many couples were doing. It would be ironic if he now had second thoughts about his proposal, while she would be ready to accept it.

She turned off College Station onto the dirt road that led to the cottage. A pair of car lights reflected in her rearview mirror. Strange that a car was behind her—and so close. There was seldom traffic on this dirt road. Some people lived farther down the road by the lake. Maybe it was one of them.

Katherine pulled into the cottage parking area, turned off the ignition, and began to open her car door. Then her heart leapt with shock. The car following her had pulled in behind her. A male figure got out and came toward her car. In the dim, interior light of her car she saw Gene's mismatched dark eyes looking in at her.

"I didn't know you lived way out here in the woods, Ms. Holiday." He began to pull the car door open wider. "Do you live alone?"

"No, I do not," she said, grasping the inside door

handle.

He held his grip on the outside. "Is your roommate at home?"

"Just leave," said Katherine. "I'm warning you."

"Warning me? Why? What are you going to do?"

The fingers of her other hand closed around her phone. "I'll call nine-one-one."

He laughed. "It would take them awhile to get way out here." Reaching in, he took her arm. Her hand fell away from the door handle; the phone fell to the floor. He was forcing her to do what she hadn't wanted to do.

"Let go, or I'll blow my car horn and my— roommate will come out."

He put his face closer to Katherine's, smiling still. "I'm not going to hurt you. We can all just have a party. Is your roommate as pretty as you?"

"My *roommate*," she said, "is Tyler McHenry."

Gene sobered for a moment. Then he said, "I'm not afraid of him." He began to pull her from the car. She blasted her car horn as he dragged her past the steering wheel. Three short beeps. Three longer ones. Three short ones. The old Morse code SOS distress signal.

Tyler must have been waiting for her in the kitchen, for in just a moment, behind the bushes separating the parking area from the cottage, a door slammed. Gene looked toward the sound and, letting her go, straightened and put his hand in his coat pocket. The branches parted, and Tyler stepped out.

Katherine saw Gene's pocketed hand grip something and begin to rise. She remembered: off campus, Gene carried a gun. Tyler's white shirt, lit up by her headlights, made him an easy target.

Katherine grabbed at Gene's arm. She had been

right. A gun dropped from his hand to the ground. At the same moment Tyler leapt from the bushes and was upon him. Gene fell. They rolled together over and over, coming to a stop with Gene on top. Gene pulled back a fist to punch Tyler, but Tyler twisted aside, rolling them again so that Gene was on the bottom. As Tyler landed his fist solidly on Gene's face, Katherine snatched up the gun and threw it into the front seat of her car. She turned back to see Tyler straddling a limp Gene. One hand was on Gene's throat, the other, balled in a fist, was raised to hit him again.

She rushed to them and grasped Tyler's raised arm. "Tyler, stop!"

It seemed he didn't hear her at first. He merely froze in position. Then he lowered his arm, turned his head, and looked at her. Slowly he removed his hand from Gene's throat, then stood and pulled Gene up, holding him by his coat lapels. "What are you doing here?"

Gene gasped hoarsely. Blood trickled from his nose. "I got lost. I didn't know you lived here."

"But you thought Katherine did. I saw you pulling her. And I saw your gun. I could have you arrested," said Tyler. "You get out of here, and I'd better not ever see you here or near Katherine again."

"Where's my gun?" Gene asked, his eyes darting nervously over the ground around them.

Katherine spoke. "It's in my car."

"And I think we'll just keep it as a souvenir," Tyler said. "It will be evidence of your visit, if we need it." He pushed Gene back to his car, parked behind Katherine's. "Now get in and get out."

Gene half fell into the car, straightened himself into the seat, and turned the key in the ignition. The car gurgled to life. He snapped the seatbelt buckle, pulled the car door shut, and backed fast out of the driveway. His glowing taillights disappeared down the road toward town.

They watched him go. Then Tyler moved to Katherine, still catching his breath. "Are you all right?"

She nodded. "I was so scared—I thought he was reaching for his gun and there you were…" She looked at him. "Should we report this to the police?"

"I think we've scared him enough. We can't prove what he *might* have done. But he could show what I did to him." Tyler wiped his forehead with his forearm, then spoke in a calmer voice. "So he followed you."

"Yes, he must have, from the Center. He has a class there again this semester."

"You can't go back there."

"I can't let him scare me away."

"Then I'm coming to class with you Thursday. I wouldn't mind sitting in your class again."

"I don't think you need to do that."

"All I know is that I am going to, this Thursday and maybe for the rest of the semester. Do you have a towel or rag in your car?"

Katherine opened the trunk and handed Tyler the towel that she kept there to wipe condensed moisture off her back windshield when she left early in the morning. He looked into her car, spotted the gun, and, encircling it with the towel, carefully picked it up. "One of those compact pistols for concealed carry," he said. "This will have your fingerprints and his on it, but it will be registered in his name. We'll keep this as evidence of his coming here armed. And he'll know we have it."

****

On Thursday, Tyler, in the desk in Classroom Six near where he'd sat before, looked at Katherine as she stood behind the lectern. He had come from work and wore the same kind of T-shirt and jeans he had worn that first day in her class. And she was wearing the turtle neck, charcoal blazer, and black slacks that he well remembered, the outfit with which she tried, without complete success, to obscure her figure. Again, he felt the tingles of physical attraction that had passed between them, unexpressed, all that past spring semester.

Neither of them had seen Gene before class. When the class was over, Tyler waited in his seat as Katherine spoke to lingering students. Then as she packed her briefcase, he went up to her lectern. They walked out of her classroom together and looked down the hall. "He's taking a class in room ten," Katherine said. They watched the students coming out of that room.

"He must not be there," said Tyler. He left Katherine's side and walked down to the classroom door, where the instructor, a tall, bespectacled young man, was just coming out. "Do you have a Gene Whittaker in this class?" Tyler asked. "I was supposed to meet him here. Maybe this is the wrong room?"

"Gene Whittaker?" the man said. "He's been in this class, but just today I received a notice that he's withdrawn."

"I see. Thank you." Tyler walked back to Katherine. "He's withdrawn from the class. Looks like we won't have to worry about Gene the rest of this semester. And I don't think we will have to worry even if he comes back in future semesters."

As they drove back to the cottage in Katherine's car, Tyler at the wheel, she felt very safe. She looked over at him as lights from oncoming cars flickered across his face. "It was strange to see you sitting there in my class again," she said.

He glanced over at her with a little smile. "Was it?"

"Do you mind?"

"Mind what?"

"That I was once your teacher. That you were my student."

"What makes you think I would mind?"

"When you asked me to marry you that time, and I didn't say yes, you thought it was because—well, you said something about my master's degree and my thinking of going on for a PhD."

Tyler's smile faded. "Did I?"

"Tyler, I admire your work, what you do. It may be dangerous but as you said, life is dangerous. I don't want you ever to think that I mind about you not going to college. I may have a BA and MA, but you've had all that amazing education from your mother." She paused. "You don't need to go back to college. You're a natural genius."

Tyler laughed a little now. "A *natural genius*?"

"It's a term I remember reading about in my British Lit class. There are natural geniuses, born with their abilities, and learned geniuses, who are taught their skills. Of course, I know it's always some of both. Your mother developed what you were born with. I guess what I'm saying, Tyler, is that you and I would not be such opposites. We're not different from each other the way your parents were."

He reached over and put his hand on her thigh. She felt its warmth through the fabric of her slacks. "No, we aren't," he said. "We make each other better."

Katherine placed her hand on top of his. Perhaps for both of them, the fear of his mother's warnings and her piercing flint-gray eyes had faded.

****

The following Monday, Katherine was in her office in Park Hall. Her day classes were over, and she planned to drink a cup of tea, grade papers for an hour or so, then head on home. She'd made spaghetti sauce the day before; she'd just heat that up and boil pasta for dinner.

Her officemate, Linda Wilson, was gathering up the materials for her next class. "I'm going out with a professor tonight."

"You are? Who?"

"He's new in the department—Spenser Johns. We met in the library a couple of weeks ago. He said he'd read over and critique the paper I'm submitting to a seminar at the MLA conference."

"Is your paper on Pope?"

Linda looked at her in surprise. "Yes. Spenser is quite an expert on Pope. In fact, he's editing a book on him. It's a collection of essays, and he might want to consider including mine." She smiled then. "I think he'll be a great contact professionally."

"And personally?"

Linda hesitated. "Right now, I'm focusing on the professional."

"I hope you can keep them separate."

Linda laughed. "Your tone is ominous. You don't think he's the campus murderer, do you?" She paused. "He did say he knew Dr. Morang."

"Really? What did he say about her?"

"They met on a faculty committee and went out a couple of times. He didn't like her. He thought she was very…unacademic."

A little wave of apprehension for Linda washed over Katherine. *Probably Dr. Morang didn't like him either.* As her officemate went out the door, she called after her, "Be careful."

Katherine swiveled her chair to her desk and sat there a moment. *I guess Linda knows what she's doing.*

She finally remembered the work awaiting her, but before tackling the first student paper in the stack, she clicked on her email. The bold print of four unread items dominated the screen.

The top one, the most recent, was from Christy. *"Can you and Tyler come over for dinner Saturday night? I'll experiment on you—I'm trying a new recipe for boeuf bourguignon."*

"We'd love being experimented on," Katherine tapped in answer, sure Tyler would agree.

The next one was from a student. *"Ms. Holiday, I'm so sorry I missed class today. I woke up with a fever and cough. My roommate will drop off my essay at your office this afternoon."*

Katherine responded, *"I hope you feel better soon. I'll be here until three. She can slide it under my door if she comes after that."*

The next was information on the Conference for College Composition and Communication, to be held in Louisville, Kentucky the following March. Katherine starred that one—she might want to submit a proposal.

When she came to the last bolded email, the name of the sender made her draw in a sharp breath. *Oh my God, Gene Whittaker.* Would this be about his fight with Tyler? Did he want his gun back? With trepidation, she clicked on it.

"*Hello, Miss Holiday. I thought you'd be interested in this article about the arborist profession published in the* Outdoor Professionals Journal." Although something told her just to delete the attachment, she opened it and read the opening paragraph:

DANGEROUS PROFESSIONS

Tree care is one of the most dangerous professions; the fatality rate is among the highest of all industries. The use of chain saws, bucket trucks, ropes and saddles, woodchippers, stump grinders and other heavy equipment as well as dealing with the intricacies of removing very heavy trees safely while working often sixty feet or more feet in the air makes the job extremely hazardous. Although most tree service jobs recommend or require some level of certification for workers, malfunctioning equipment is also a danger and there is little government oversight in that area. The ISA (International Society of Arboriculture) newsletter lists numerous accidents and deaths in the profession every month.

She snapped the attachment closed and deleted the email. What was that crazy Gene trying to do? Frighten her? Cause problems in her relationship with Tyler? The article made Tyler's mother's warnings about the dangers of the profession rise up again.

Or was the email an indirect threat to Tyler?

I will forget this. She picked up the first student essay and began to read. But she noted that her hand was slightly shaking.

"Tyler," she said that night in bed, "is being an arborist really so dangerous?"

"What?" he rose up on his elbow and looked down

at her, with that smile of his. "Where did that question come from?"

"I've just been thinking."

"We've been over this before. So now, all I'll say is—what's that line? 'Don't you worry your pretty little head about it.' " He leaned over and kissed her.

What ensued left no opportunity for further conversation.

****

They had both gone to sleep afterward—and then the buzz of Tyler's phone on the table beside the bed awoke them. Tyler reached out and answered. Katherine lifted her head sleepily. "What time is it?"

"Two o'clock." Tyler put the phone to his ear. "Hello, Dad. Is something wrong?" He listened. His voice became tense. "Did you call the police? Don't go out until they come. I'll be right over. I should get there in fifteen minutes." He hung up and reached for his clothes discarded on a chair by the bed.

"What is it?" Katherine asked.

"Someone must have broken into the equipment shed. The alarm went off. The police will be coming, but I'm afraid Dad might go out to the shed by himself. I'm going over there." He pulled on his jeans, his sweatshirt.

"Tyler! I need to tell you something."

"What?"

"This is probably not related, but I got an email from Gene Whittaker yesterday afternoon. He sent me an article about the dangers of tree cutting and... malfunctioning equipment."

Tyler froze for a moment. "Oh, he did, did he?"

"I thought you should know."

"Yes, I should. Stay here, keep the doors locked."

He opened the dresser drawer and stuck something, wrapped in a piece of cloth, into his belt. Then he gave her a quick kiss and was gone. It was only then she realized: he'd taken Gene's gun.

Fully awake now, Katherine got out of bed, pulled on her nightgown, put on her slippers and bathrobe. The November night was chilly. Tyler had turned the outdoor lights on; they lit the yard outside up to the hedge dividing the lawn from the parking area. Everything was quiet except for a barred owl hooting occasionally out in the woods. She checked to be sure all the doors were locked, then walked to the kitchen. She poured herself a glass of sherry and sat at the table there, sipping. Surely it was just coincidence that the night after Gene sent that email, the alarm had gone off in the McHenry storage shed. Was Tyler in danger?

She drained her glass of sherry and got up to put it in the sink when she heard a *clink* outside. She stood still as a statue and listened. Nothing, just the *whoo* of the barred owl. Then…another *clink*.

If someone was out there in the dark, they could see her through the windows. She turned out the kitchen light and went back to their bedroom. There she picked up her phone, turned out the light by the bed, and sat down. Maybe Tyler would call. Even as she had that thought, her phone lit up and buzzed. But it was not Tyler—an unfamiliar number came up on the screen. She stared at it. Better not to answer.

The buzzing ceased. Maybe the caller would leave a message. After a moment she went to voice mail. "One unheard message," said the voice. Gene's voice came on. *"Good evening, Ms. Holiday, or I guess I should say good morning. I just wondered if you were all right. I understand the police were called to McHenry Tree Service about two this morning. I hope there was no damage to the equipment there. I see Tyler's truck is gone. So no roommate with you now, Ms. Holiday?"*

He must be outside to know that Tyler's truck was gone—or did he just guess? Chills of fear went through Katherine. Gene was not just a pest after all. He seemed a real danger. She punched the emergency number on the phone, hoping the police would not consider her just a hysterical female.

"Nine-one-one," came a female voice.

"I think someone is prowling outside my house," Katherine said. "He just called me. He knew one of our vehicles was not here, that my—boyfriend was gone."

"Is this someone you're afraid of?"

She hesitated. "Yes."

"We'll send a unit out," the dispatcher said. "What's your address?"

After she disconnected, she sat in the dark and waited. She knew, as Gene had pointed out that night he followed her home, that it would take a while for the police to get there. Her phone buzzed and lit up again, displaying the same number as before. This time she answered.

"You didn't need to do that," Gene's voice said.

"Do what?"

"Call the police."

"How did you know I did?"

"I have a police radio in my car."

She breathed a little easier. "Is that how you knew about the break-in at the McHenry garage?"

"Did you think I was the one that broke in?"

"I thought maybe."

He laughed. "You give me a lot of credit, Miss Holiday."

But he had known Tyler's truck was gone. "Where are you?"

"I'm sitting on your porch steps."

Her heart began to race. "The police will be coming."

"Yes, I'd better leave. I was going to tell them I came to retrieve some stolen property, but I suppose they'd wonder why I came at this time of night. So good night, Ms. Holiday. I'll try again later. I suppose you'll give them my name."

"Yes, I will."

He disconnected. She went to the window and looked out but saw nothing. He must have parked out on the road. Maybe he wasn't on her steps at all but sitting in his car somewhere far away listening to the police radio and guessing about Tyler's being gone. He'd just wanted to scare her.

Then she heard the sounds of an engine turn over in their parking area. A gleam of lights shone through the bushes as a car backed out and headed down the road toward the highway.

****

Tyler charged through the porch door and into the kitchen where Katherine sat at the table with a male and female police officer. "What happened? What's wrong?"

The police officers stood. The woman held out her hand. "Officer Marty Jenkins here," she said. "This is my partner Josh Neighbors. You must be Tyler McHenry."

Tyler took her hand, then Officer Neighbors', then turned to Katherine. "Are you all right?"

Officer Jenkins answered for her. "It looks like it's

a case of possible stalking here." She looked at her notes. "We understand that a Gene Whittaker, a former student of Miss Holiday's, followed her here from campus last Tuesday with a gun and sent her what could be considered a threatening email yesterday. Tonight, he has called her twice, possibly trespassing on this property."

"Damn!" said Tyler

"We will be investigating to hear his side of the story," said Officer Neighbors. "In the meantime, will you want to file for a restraining order on this individual?"

"Absolutely."

"Miss Holiday?"

"How will that stop him?" asked Katherine.

"If we put such an order on him and he then attempts any of these behaviors again, the offense will be elevated to aggravated stalking, which is a felony. If he's found guilty, the penalty will be a prison term of one to ten years and a fine of up to ten thousand dollars."

Tyler sat down at the table then, as did the officers. "There's something you should know," he said. "My father and I own a tree service. Tonight the alarm went off in the building where we store our vehicles and equipment, but all we could find was a broken window. That must have set off the alarm. Katherine got the calls from Whittaker while I was gone. He might be responsible for the alarm going off."

"It's possible. You say no intruder actually entered the storage building?"

"We found no evidence that anyone had."

"If there is a connection, and even if there's not, what would be Mr. Whittaker's motivation in all this?"

asked Officer Neighbors.

"I think he's trying to scare me—us," said Katherine.

Tyler spoke. "Ms. Holiday was his teacher last spring semester in a UGA evening class. I think he has some kind of crush on her. She's let him know that she doesn't want him bothering her."

"And what is *your* relationship with Ms. Holiday?" asked Officer Jenkins.

"We live together," said Katherine quickly. This was going to get tricky. What if Gene tells of Tyler's hitting him, of taking his gun?

But her answer seemed enough for them. "All right." The officers stood. Officer Neighbors spoke. "You will need to file documents at the county courthouse for the restraining order. You can get them online. A hearing will be scheduled at which the defendant, Mr. Whittaker, will have the opportunity to present his side of the case. Then the judge will decide if a restraining order should be issued."

The female officer added, "For now, we'll follow up with Mr. Whittaker, check on his movements tonight. You showed us a copy of that email he sent you yesterday. If you go ahead with filing for a restraining order, you will want to bring copies of that email, his voice mail, tonight's police report, and notes on his following you here two days ago, as well as any other related events to the hearing. For now, stay safe. Don't go anywhere alone, especially at night. Keep your doors locked. Good night."

"Good night. Thank you," said Katherine. She and Tyler went with them to the door.

Chapter Ten

Katherine turned to Tyler, who was locking the front door. "You took Gene's gun with you tonight?"

"Yes—I wore my work gloves so I wouldn't get my fingerprints on it. I locked it in the truck when I saw the police cars. I thought I might need it at the storage shed. Like I told the officers, though, it turned out to be just the broken window."

"Do you think Gene broke it?"

"He might have hoped setting off the alarm there would get me away from the house. And then he could have come over here and called you. He didn't do any real harm other than scare you, but I think we have enough evidence to have a restraining order put on him. I'll show his gun at the hearing if I have to, though I'd rather not. He'd claim he always carried it and didn't pull it on us. I might look bad for keeping it, though I'd tell them why I did."

"I hate to go through a hearing," said Katherine. "I'd hoped he'd just go away."

"He's obviously a little crazy," said Tyler. "There just are people like that out there in the world." He put his arms around her. "Let's try to get some sleep. I have to work in a few hours. It's lucky you don't have a class until the evening."

"I don't want you up in the bucket when you're tired."

"I'll be all right. Come on." He led her back to their bedroom, where, in the bed, he folded her in his arms. His warmth comforted her.

That evening when she got home from her Tuesday class Tyler told her, "I filled out the restraining order request forms today and sent them to the county office."

"Maybe we shouldn't be so paranoid about Gene," Katherine replied. "I think he will stay away from us now that the police have talked to him."

But on Tuesday and Thursday evenings, Tyler was always waiting at the door, watchful, when she returned.

****

As the days went by, Katherine began to breathe more easily. Surely, she thought, the police checking on Gene's whereabouts the night of his phone calls had frightened him enough. The hearing for the restraining order was set for December fifteenth. The semester's classes came to an end on December eighth, followed by the usual grading of the take-home essay exams and the filing of grades.

The next week, trying to put aside thoughts of Gene, Katherine and Tyler went to a tree farm and cut their own Christmas tree, decorating it with old-fashioned ornaments purchased at the Potter's House. Tyler went out on their property and cut greenery—cedar boughs and smilax—for the mantel and stairs. They invited Tyler's father to dinner one night, then Christy, Tom, Marian, and Wilson. Life began to feel normal.

"Do you really think we need to go through with this restraining order?" Katherine asked Tyler as they sat together on the couch one evening soon after, a fire in the fireplace, wine glasses in their hands.

"You really don't want to, do you?" Tyler said.

"We haven't heard from Gene. I think it's over."

"You sure it's not just the Christmas spirit—and this wine—making you mellow?"

"The hearing would ruin Christmas. We'd have to see him there. Please, Tyler, let's not go through with it. The police have talked to him. That should be enough."

"All right, then. We'll cancel on one condition—that you promise if he contacts you in any way again, we'll go through with a restraining order after all."

She hesitated, then nodded. "All right, I promise."

****

The next day Katherine sat in a booth at the Hilltop Restaurant waiting for her friend Marian. "I need to talk to you about something," Marian had said earlier. That was all. Katherine was curious.

Maybe it was about a newspaper story Marian was working on? Or maybe she and Wilson were getting married? A Christmas carol played softly in the background and a fire blazed in the stone fireplace near their booth. In its warmth Katherine shrugged off her jacket.

Marian appeared. "Hi!"

Katherine looked up with a smile, but it faded when she saw Marian's serious expression. "You look worried," she said.

"I don't know if I should be or not." Marian slid into the booth opposite Katherine and pulled out her phone. "I got this email with an embedded photo this morning. It mentions you." She clicked on the phone, pulled up the image, and shoved the phone across the table. Katherine picked it up and looked down at the screen. Gene's face with a blackened eye and blood crusted nose filled the lighted rectangle.

Above the photo was the message, "November 5, 2009. Your friend Katherine Holiday might be interested in this photo."

"The name on the email is just 'appboy.' Do you know who that is?" Marian asked.

Katherine studied the picture. "He…he might have been a student of mine. This is all? No other message?"

"No. It looks like a selfie. And he's been hurt. What do you think it's all about?"

Katherine shook her head. But she knew. November fifth was the evening he had followed her to the cottage and Tyler had fought with him. Gene was showing her, without contacting her directly, that he had evidence against Tyler that could be shown at the hearing for the restraining order. He didn't know she and Tyler had decided to drop the request. Well, he'd hear soon enough.

Marian persisted. "He may have learned we were friends from my Facebook page or something, but why would he send me this picture? Why would he want me to show it to you?"

"I don't know."

Marian took back her phone. "It doesn't make sense. Maybe this is something for a newspaper story. I guess I should answer his email and find out. But I thought I'd check with you first."

"I think you should wait," said Katherine. "Look at his eyes. He looks strange. It's not a good idea to answer weird emails like this."

"Maybe for most people. But I'm a reporter."

"Well, just wait and see if he contacts you again with more information," said Katherine. "Please, Marian."

Marian eyed her suspiciously. "I think you know

more about this than you're telling me."

"All right, he was in my evening class last spring. And he followed me home once this fall."

"Is that all? Nothing more?"

"No, not really."

Marian tapped her phone screen. "I don't suppose you did *this* to him for following you home."

Katherine laughed too, hoping she didn't sound nervous. "If I had, I wouldn't worry about him hurting you. You're tougher than I am."

Marian put the phone in her purse. "All right, I'll wait and see if he contacts me again. It may be just a student prank. In both our professions, we sometimes run into cranks." She looked up as the waiter approached. "I think we both need some Merlot—right, Katherine?"

****

Christmas celebrations began to fill Katherine's mind. Surely Gene had just been letting her know what he would show at the hearing, and now that there was no hearing, the issue of the photo was moot. There were parties: one for the McHenry tree crew at Tyler's father's, one given by Marian, who said she'd heard nothing more from Gene, one given by Christy and Tom, and an English department party at Dr. Flatt's.

The pre-Christmas season ended with the dramatic candlelight Christmas Eve ceremony at the First Presbyterian Church. Tyler's father spent Christmas day with them, and she and Tyler spent the three following days hiking in the North Carolina mountains, wearing the down-filled jackets they had given each other for Christmas.

Back at home, Tyler began working again with the tree service by day, while Katherine spent time in her home office getting ready for the next semester of classes. This time she was teaching two sections of sophomore literature and two composition classes—one in the day, one, as usual, to adults in the evenings. At night Tyler was beginning to write again, sitting at his laptop in his upstairs office.

"A second novel?" she asked, stopping at his office door on one of those evenings.

"We don't know if I even have a first novel," he said. "But I have to put down what is coming into my head."

She remembered his writing sessions until early morning on the coffee table in his doublewide. "I hope this novel won't take you away from me too much at night."

He turned in his swivel chair and regarded her with his smile. "I don't think you have to worry about that."

She went back downstairs and into their large bedroom at the end of the hall. Turning back the covers, she climbed in and lay there. Should she turn out the light? She must have dozed before deciding, for suddenly she was awakened by a warm body rolling in next to her, and gentle arms taking hold of her.

"Hi, lady."

She opened her eyes and smiled. Without speaking she reached up and put her arms around his neck, as he slid his hands up under her flannel nightgown.

****

The winter-spring semester classes began. Gene was apparently not taking any classes. Katherine was glad; the January evenings were dusky when she arrived at her adult class on Tuesdays and Thursdays, and it was fully night when she got home. She had supper before she left, and Tyler began eating with his father on those nights, but was back by the time she returned.

On the Tuesday evening of the third week of classes, however, Tyler's truck was not in the parking area when she turned in. Hoping nothing was wrong, she walked back to the cottage carrying her briefcase. She was about to unlock the screen door when a dark figure strolled around from the back of the house. "Hello, Katherine."

She turned to face it. Of course. Somehow, though she'd tried to deny it, she'd suspected this meeting would occur sometime. "Hello, Gene."

"I appreciated you dropping the restraining order."

"We thought it wasn't needed. Maybe we were wrong."

"I'm not stalking or harassing you. I just stopped by to get back my property."

"Your gun?"

"Yes. I need it back."

"Tyler only kept it in case we needed to show it to the police sometime."

"I wasn't going to use it that night. I just had my hand on it in my pocket. You made me drop it."

"It was hard to tell what you were going to do."

"I guess you saw the picture of what your friend Tyler did to me that night."

"Yes. Marian showed it to me."

"I thought the judge might be interested in that if it ever came to a hearing on the restraining order. But you've cancelled your application. So if you give me my gun now, I'll never bother you again."

"You'll have to deal with Tyler about that. I don't know where he put it."

"I think you do." He grabbed her arm suddenly, like

a serpent striking. Her briefcase fell to the step. "Unlock the door, Ms. Holiday. We're going inside to get it." He took the keys from her fisted hand and, noting the one she had separated from the others, unlocked the screen door. As he pulled her onto the porch and began looking through the keys for the one to the kitchen door, she noted that he was wearing gloves. Katherine reached out with her free hand and knocked the keys to the floor.

"Oh, you're sneaky that way, are you?" He pinned her against the door. "But no Tyler here to beat me up this time."

"Did you do something to make him late?"

He did not answer that. Instead, holding her with his wiry arms, he kissed her hard on the mouth even as she pushed against him. Finally, he drew back. "I've been wanting to do that for a long time. You'd understand if you'd read my poem. I wanted that more than I wanted the gun."

"Then now you can leave."

He shook his head. "Like I said, I need the gun." He kept one hand on the door beside her, bent down and swooped up the keys, fanned them out, selected one. "This looks like the type for this door." He inserted it, turned it, and the lock clicked. He pushed the door open and holding her arm twisted behind her, shoved her inside. "Okay, where is it?"

"Will you leave if I give it to you?"

"Yes."

"Then go back out on the porch and I'll throw it out to you."

"Hah, I wouldn't trust you on that. Take me to it." He gave her arm a jerk. "And don't tell me you don't know where it is."

"You know I'll report this to the police."

"You won't have to. I told you—give me the gun and you'll never see me again."

"Then let go of me."

He dropped her arm. She rubbed it to get the circulation going again. "I think it's in our bedroom."

"Ah, a good place. I'll follow you. And maybe I should tell you—I have another gun with me. Just in case."

Katherine didn't know whether the gun she'd seen Tyler get out of the drawer had been put back there, and if so, if it was still loaded. But she felt she didn't have much choice but to look. She walked to the bedroom, Gene close behind her.

"Hurry up," he said.

"I told you—I'm not sure where Tyler put it. He may have it in his truck." She opened one of his drawers, looked under the piled underwear. If she found it, could she take it, point it at Gene? But she didn't even know if it was loaded or how to shoot. She felt the hard object at the bottom of the second pile of underwear. Seeing her hesitate, Gene reached in and grabbed at it. It was indeed his gun.

"Thank you," he said. He took it up, checked it. "Ah, still loaded and ready to go."

"Now that you have it, get out of here," said Katherine.

They heard the crunch of a vehicle driving into the pebbled parking area. Gene raised his head in surprise. Then he said, "Ah, too late. Your *roommate* is back. This isn't something I planned on."

The truck door slammed, and in a moment, hurried footsteps came up the steps to the porch, then inside.

Gene held Katherine against him, both of them facing the bedroom door, the loaded gun he'd just taken pointed toward it. "I could make this look like a murder-suicide, you know," he said.

Katherine cried out, "Tyler—stay away!"

The footsteps paused, then came on. The bedroom door opened, and she caught a brief glimpse of Tyler standing there. With lightning quickness, he grabbed Katherine's makeup mirror on the dressing table next to the door and hurled it at Gene's head. It hit its mark even as the gun went off. Katherine screamed, terrified that Tyler had been hit. But as blood poured down from Gene's scalp, Tyler ran to him, snatched the gun and pointed it at him.

"He's got another gun," Katherine said.

"Search his pockets and find it."

She patted Gene's first jacket pocket, felt the metal object right away, and pulled another handgun out.

"Throw it on the bed, get my phone out of my back pocket, and call nine-one-one."

Shaken, Katherine threw the gun to the bed, pulled Tyler's phone out, and punched the emergency number. "Come right away. There's been an intruder, a shooting." She gave the address, clicked off, and looked at Tyler. Blood was staining his jacket sleeve a bright red. "Oh, God, you've been hit."

"Just my arm," said Tyler.

"My eyes," said Gene, his face covered in blood. "I can't see."

Katherine looked at Tyler. "Shall I get some towels?"

"Yes. He needs to wipe himself off. And I need one for a tourniquet."

Katherine rushed to the bathroom, grabbed two towels, returned and handed one to Gene who held it to his head. Then she helped Tyler take off his jacket even as he continued to hold the gun on Gene. She tied the second towel tight around the bicep of his injured arm.

"Sit down," Tyler ordered Gene, indicating a chair, and when Gene obeyed, he sat in another one. "We'll have a little wait. This goes beyond a restraining order now, Whittaker. You'll be behind bars."

"I think I can tell them a pretty convincing story. I was just here to get some stolen property."

"But hard evidence is what's important. Remember my class?" said Katherine.

"I'll always remember your class, honey," said Gene. The blood wiped away, he wrapped the towel around his head and looked at her with his strange eyes. "If you'd just treated me equally, none of this would have happened." He looked over at the bed. "I bet you two have some good times there."

"Maybe you'd better just stop talking," said Tyler.

"I'll take his gun to the kitchen. I don't like seeing it," said Katherine. She picked it up, then paused. "Will you be all right, Tyler?"

"Yes, just get rid of that gun."

Katherine went out to the kitchen and laid it on the counter. She heard a loud thump from the bedroom and remembering the fight in the men's rest room, rushed back. Tyler's chair had been tipped over, and he was on the floor—apparently Gene had tried to rush him—but Tyler still was pointing the gun at Gene. "Don't make me shoot you," he said.

Katherine set the chair upright and helped Tyler into it. Gene sat back in his own chair.

"So *you* were the one who slashed my tires," Tyler said. "I guess you didn't figure we had plenty of spares in the storage shed."

"No," said Gene. "I didn't figure that."

They heard sirens in the distance. "They'll be here in a minute," Katherine said.

Gene looked at them. "Don't give that gun to the police."

"I'll have to," said Tyler.

The sirens shrilled louder, and cars crunched into the pebbled parking area. The sirens blipped off, doors slammed. Hurried steps came into the house. "Mr. McHenry? Ms. Holiday?" a man's voice called.

"We're in here," replied Katherine. Three policemen appeared in the open bedroom door.

"Here's your man," said Tyler. "He came here and threatened Katherine. He shot at me."

"And hit you," commented one of the cops, eyeing Tyler's arm. He looked around. "And then your bedroom doorframe. You've got a nice bullet hole there."

"This is his gun—the one he shot with. He had another one. Katherine took it to the kitchen."

The first police officer turned to one of the others and motioned toward Tyler. "Take that gun and get the one in the kitchen. We'd better get Mr. McHenry to the emergency room." He then looked at Gene, blood soaking through the towel around his head. "Both of them. That one'll need stitches."

He hauled Gene to his feet and handcuffed him. After reciting the Miranda warning, they began to take him from the room. At the door, Gene turned to Tyler and Katherine. "Well," he said, with a kind of smile, "I guess I'll see you in court after all."

169

****

While Tyler was taken to the hospital for treatment, the third officer remained to take photographs, extract the bullet from the doorframe, and ask Katherine a series of questions. She told him the full story of their keeping the gun when Gene first came to their house.

The questions over, she went to pick Tyler up. She found him sitting on the bed in a small emergency treatment room, a thick white bandage around his arm. As she entered, he stood, arms open.

"I'm so sorry. This was all my fault." She walked into his embrace, not fighting the beginning tears.

"I'd say it was Gene's fault," said Tyler. He stepped back. "Anyway, I've given my report to the police. I guess you have too."

She nodded.

"You told them again about Gene following you home that night—and also about our fight and my keeping his gun?"

"Yes."

"So did I. Our stories will match. I think tonight, bad as he is, he mainly wanted to get his gun. I just surprised him, coming back and throwing that mirror."

"What did the doctor say about your arm?"

"There may have been a lot of blood, but the bullet just grazed it. I'll be fine."

"But it hit the doorframe where you were standing. That was so close." She shook her head. "I should never have asked to cancel that restraining order."

"He could have come here even if there had been one. Honey, I've told you—there are risks in every profession." He picked up his jacket. "They're about to discharge me, and we can go home. They'll book Gene into jail. He shouldn't be a problem for us anymore. Let's try to forget this and look ahead. Okay?"

She nodded, fished a tissue from her purse, and wiped her eyes as a doctor knocked perfunctorily on the door. "Here is the instruction sheet," he said as he entered, "and a prescription for pain killers, though you may not need any, and an antibiotic. You were lucky, young man."

"I know," said Tyler. He signed the sheet the doctor offered him and accepted the copy of the instructions. He and Katherine walked together to the checkout office, then out of the hospital and to her car.

"You know what you have to worry about now?" Tyler said, as they settled in and fastened their seat belts.

Katherine drew in a breath. "What?"

"When we'll hear something about my book."

Katherine smiled then. "I won't worry about that. It's just a matter of time."

Chapter Eleven

Tyler himself had a plan that he'd wanted for some time to act on—something he didn't want Katherine to know about. After what happened with Gene, he didn't want to wait any longer. The next week on a Thursday afternoon he took a ring from her drawer and went to a jewelry store in downtown Athens.

"I want to buy an engagement ring," he said to the old clerk who approached him. He laid Katherine's ring on the counter. "This is the size."

"How much do you want to spend?"

"Just show me some." He looked over the diamond rings laid out before him. He wanted something graceful and tasteful—like Katherine herself. "Here is a nice one," said the man, pointing. "Those double diamonds are quite spectacular, aren't they? That ring is five thousand dollars."

Tyler looked down at it, but the diamonds in the ring the man pointed to seemed almost too large, even gawdy, and he knew Katherine would rather spend that much money in some other way. There was another ring that caught his eye, a simple silver band with a single diamond. "What about that one?"

"That's a six-prong round cut Tiffany style. The band is fourteen carat white gold, and it's tapered to make it fit comfortably. The diamond is one-carat—and good quality. See how clear it is?" He held it up.

"How much is it?"

The clerk smiled. "You're in luck. It was sixteen hundred dollars, but it's on sale for twelve hundred."

"I like it," said Tyler. "You have it in her size?"

"Yes, we do. I'll package it up for you if that's your choice."

Tyler looked again at it and knew. "Yes, sir," he said. "It is."

A gray-haired woman examining china patterns at the next counter looked over at him and then at the ring. "Oh, how sweet," she said. "I'm sure she'll love it. I wish you a long and happy marriage."

"Thank you, ma'am," Tyler replied, embarrassed.

"So many marriages fail these days. I think of that poor woman professor at the university whose husband killed her."

"What?" said Tyler. "I thought they hadn't solved that murder."

"They haven't, but it seems to me quite clear. He's the only person of interest they've been questioning repeatedly over all these months. He must have known she was having some relationships after she left him, and he was jealous. I'm sure he came to her building and saw her through the window in that elevator, coming down maybe with a man. And," she finished, with a kind of relish, "when the man left, he killed her."

"Ah, Mrs. Simpson, you read too many murder mysteries," said the clerk. "I just heard the latest in the real story from my detective friend who stopped in this afternoon. They have someone they are going to charge—and it's not her husband. It's one of Dr. Morang's Psychology Clinic clients. They'd questioned him right after her murder—like they did all of her students and clients—but even though he had no witnesses to back up where he said he was the night of the murder, they didn't find anything particularly suspicious about him. Then last week he was arrested on an aggravated assault charge involving a shooting, so they began questioning him again about the murder. He still denied any knowledge of it, of course, but they'd confiscated two guns from him in that arrest. Back in the lab, when they checked the tool marks on the bullets in Dr. Morang's body against bullets fired from his guns, the marks on one of his guns were a positive match. That was the gun that killed her. And they checked the dates he bought and registered that gun. He owned it at the time of her murder."

"Did your friend tell you this guy's name?" asked Tyler.

"Maybe I shouldn't say—but there will be a police conference tomorrow and it will be on the news. I think it was Gene something—Gene Whitting, Whitstone— something like that."

"Are you all right, young man?" the woman asked.

"Yes, yes," said Tyler. "Just…just box up the ring for me, sir. Here is my credit card."

****

"Tyler, what's the matter?" asked Katherine that night when she got home from her evening classes. He had hugged her tightly and seemed not to want to leave her side.

"I'm just glad you're here," Tyler said. "I've made a mac and cheese casserole for a late dinner. And here's a glass of wine."

She smiled a little at his word "casserole." She'd taught him to layer his mac and cheese with slices of ham, and they both now used that term for his dish. But she waved aside the stemmed glass he held out to her. "I don't want any wine tonight."

"You'd better have some. Sit down. I have something to tell you." He put the glass down before her at the table. He looked serious.

She sat. "Is something wrong?"

"I'm not sure. Maybe it could be considered good news. Come on, drink up."

Katherine took a sip as she watched Tyler down his in quick swallows. "Are you reverting to the chug-a-lug method of drinking?"

He did not even smile. "There's going to be a police news conference tomorrow. The police think they've found the person who killed Dr. Morang. We know him."

She stopped with her glass midway to her lips. "Who?"

"Gene Whittaker."

"*Gene?* But he didn't even know Dr. Morang."

"Turns out he did. The UGA Psychology Clinic provides low-cost services to anyone in the Athens community. Grad students in the clinical psych program get training there under the supervision of faculty. Gene was a client at the clinic, and she supervised the grad student working with him. It's not surprising Gene was getting help, is it? He isn't right."

"Why do they think he was Dr. Morang's killer?"

"The evidence sounds pretty strong. I guess after they arrested Gene here last week and ran a check on him, his name again came up as one of the Psychology Clinic clients linked to Dr. Morang. So they took bullets fired from his two guns, including the bullet from our doorframe—and compared the tool marks on them against the ones that killed Dr. Morang. The marks on bullets from the gun he shot me with were a match."

"So that means Gene killed her?"

"It means Gene's gun killed her—the one he brought to our house on November fifth. But it's pretty clear. The timelines suggest he owned that gun at the time of her murder. And he has no alibi for that night."

"Oh, my God, Dr. Morang's murderer was in my class all last spring semester!"

"Yes, right there, a student in Classroom Six with us all." Tyler poured himself another glass of wine. "I can imagine what happened. Since Dr. Morang supervised the grad student he was working with, she sometimes saw Gene herself. He developed sexual fantasies about her—the way he must have about you. He approached her, and she rejected him. His anger and jealousy— maybe of that grad student—built up. He must have known her work habits. He came to campus with his gun late that night, saw her coming down in the elevator. He approached her again and, when she rejected him, he killed her."

His voice quavered just a little then. "That first night when he followed you home, he might have done that to you if I hadn't been there—and he might have last week if I hadn't come back when I did."

Katherine stood and wrapped her arms around him. "He could have killed us both then. When he heard you coming in, he said something about making it look like a murder-suicide."

"We'll both have to testify at his trial if he doesn't plead guilty. But if there is a trial, I think the evidence is strong enough we won't need to worry about the verdict. Anyway, life can get back to normal now—for us and for

176

the campus." He pulled back and spoke gently. "So…have you lost your appetite, or will you eat some of my casserole?"

Katherine smiled a little. Her voice was weak, but she said, "I'll eat some of your casserole."

****

On a cold night in mid-January Tyler, looking up at Katherine from the stone fireplace where he was building a fire, said. "Hey, your birthday is coming up. How should we celebrate?"

She laughed. "How about something original—maybe a cake?"

"I should bake one?"

"You could use a mix."

"Let's ask Christy and Tom and Marian and Wilson for dinner that night," said Tyler. "I'll make my mac and cheese casserole to go with the cake."

"And we can drink beer," said Katherine. "Like at the tailgate."

"Sounds like a plan," said Tyler. As the fire flared up, he stood and seemed to think a moment. "But right now, I want to show you something. An email came in just a few minutes ago. Come to my office." He led her upstairs to his computer, sat down, and tapped at the keyboard.

"What is it?" Katherine leaned over and read aloud: "*Mr. McHenry, I am delighted to inform you that Stonelake Press is interested in publishing your novel. You will receive a check for ten thousand dollars, your advance, should you decide to sign the attached contract. Please look it over carefully. I will be glad to answer any questions you have. Kitty Harding, agent.*"

She looked up. "That's a prestigious press!"

"I thought of waiting to show you this for your birthday, but I couldn't."

She hugged him ecstatically. "I would never have forgiven you if you hadn't told me right away." She paused. "We'll have to look over the contract, maybe confer with a lawyer. And then if you decide to sign, we can tell everyone. My birthday party can celebrate your book too."

****

Late in the afternoon of Katherine's birthday, January twenty-sixth, she heard sounds of a large vehicle pulling up into their parking area. Tyler was getting home earlier during these short days, but it did not sound like his truck. Pulling on her heavy sweater, she emerged through the bushes to see the company's biggest bucket truck being maneuvered onto the grass at the side of the pebbled parking area. Tyler got out of the cab.

"What is that doing here?" Katherine asked. The big machines were normally kept at Tyler's father's storage building behind his house.

"I told Dad I'd park it here and take it directly to the work site tomorrow morning," said Tyler. "The site is not far from here."

"But will there be room for Christy and Marian to park for the party?"

"Oh sure, there's plenty of room. I parked way over on the grass." Tyler came to her side. "Going to your class that time last semester gave me an idea. For your birthday, let's do something else—something for old time's sake."

"What?"

"Take another ride in the bucket truck." His voice lowered. "Remember your first one?"

"Of course, Tyler. But our company will be coming any minute and you were going to cook—"

"You can see a wonderful view from here—the lake, the woods, the sunset."

Giving her no further chance to protest, he led her to the truck and followed her up the steps to the platform, where he boosted her into the bucket and got in himself. He stood behind her as he fastened safety harnesses around them and started the engine attached to the bucket. His arms on each side of her as before, he moved the gears on the instrument panel. Katherine quieted. She loved being tethered near him like this, and the sensation of rising…rising…rising with him. She looked down, speechless, at the beauty of the now bare tree branches, the lake, the roof of their little cottage tucked into the woods. At seventy feet, the bucket stopped and hung there in the air like a car on a carnival ride.

"Would you like to steer the bucket?" he asked.

She turned part way around and looked up at Tyler. "You know I can't."

"Just look at the instrument panel—at the lever on the far right."

Katherine looked toward it, then froze. Beside the lever, in an open little velvet box, was a ring, its diamond sparkling in the rays of the setting sun. "Oh, Tyler, it's beautiful!"

As she looked at it, his hand came forward, plucked the ring from the box, and held it to her finger. "I'll do it right this time. I can't kneel here, but"—his voice became formal—"Ms. Holiday, will you marry me?"

This time she did not hesitate. "Yes, Mr. McHenry, I will."

He slid the ring onto her finger. "Happy birthday."

And against the background of luminous pink clouds and the setting winter sun, he kissed her. As he lifted his head, Katherine heard some noises below. It sounded like cheering. She looked down. Three cars were now parked in the pebbled area below, and six small human figures were waving up at them. It was Christy, Tom, Marian and Wilson, and Tyler's father, his hand on the arm of a woman she did not know.

"Everyone's here," she said. "And your father too! He's with someone."

"Oh, that's Mrs. Peters—she's a widow who wanted to go back to work. Dad hired her as our business secretary. She'll answer the calls, take care of the scheduling and billing. It was getting to be too much for Dad and me with all the actual tree work. I suggested he bring her tonight."

"What a good idea to hire a secretary," said Katherine. *It may be a good idea for your father in other ways too.* "Her help will be great. You'll have more time to do edits and publicity for your novel…and work on that next book."

He nuzzled her cheek. "And how about travel? I want to go to some of the world's famous forests, in California, Germany, the Amazon. And all over the United States, England and Europe, Asia, Africa, places my mother taught me about."

"Yes, we'll travel," said Katherine. Then she pulled back. "But Tyler, I can arrange my schedule for trips during vacations if I go on for a PhD, but can you leave the business long enough to travel?"

"I can arrange to take one big trip a year."

Katherine thought a moment more. "But someday we may have a baby."

"When we do, we'll take him traveling with us."

"Him?"

"Him or her!"

Katherine laughed and snuggled back against him. "At first, in one of those backpacks," she said.

She heard another car pull into the parking area. Down on the ground a couple got out of it, looked up at them, and waved. "Who can that be?" she asked. "Oh, Tyler—it's my parents!"

"Yes, they flew down and rented a car," said Tyler. "Everyone's here to celebrate your birthday and my book, and they hoped they'd be celebrating something else, too. So it's a good thing this time when I proposed you said yes. By the way, Christy and Tom have brought Spanish paella and wine for dinner—a much better spread for your birthday. And for dessert, Marian and Wilson brought a cake from Celine's Bakery—they make the best cakes in town."

"You planned all this?"

"Right down to the timing. Everyone was to arrive here just about sunset—when I planned to take you up in the bucket and make a proper proposal."

"It was a perfect proposal," said Katherine. They kissed again. Then they leaned over the edge of the bucket and waved joyously to the group below. The future at that moment seemed only safe, bright, and promising.

"Time to go back to earth," Tyler said.

She turned to face away from him as, his arms on each side of her, he put his hands on the instrument panel. He felt warm and solid against her as they descended.

Author's Note

While this novel is set in Athens, Georgia, often at the University of Georgia, some details of this setting are changed. I invented the Continuing Education Center. By 2009, the year most of this novel takes place, undergraduate evening classes for UGA credit were no longer offered—and even when they had been, they were not part of faculty members' regular assignments, as they are in the novel. Class evaluations were still done by hand, however, and essays were still printed and handed in to the teachers in hard copy—though in this story I have the final exam sent in by email. An outside elevator does exist at UGA's Psychology-Journalism building, but it has no windows. Oconee Forest is based on the Warnell School of Forestry's Oconee Forest Park, but it is imaginary, as are Tyler's cottage, the road on which it is located, the Dark Owl Lounge, and Harry's Bar. Finally, of course, all the characters and incidents are fictional.

I owe much gratitude to my editor, Kaycee John; my sister, Dorothy Altman; my friend Jane Marston; and my husband, Hubert McAlexander, for their advice and support as I wrote and revised this novel. I am also grateful to arborist Shawn Doonan of New Urban Forestry in Athens, who offered advice regarding his profession as well as an opportunity to visit a work site and talk with the crew.

I love to hear from my readers. Email me at mcalexanderpatricia@gmail.com or follow me on Facebook. And take a look at my website: https://patriciamcalexander.weebly.com.

Finally, please, please rate and review this novel on Amazon, Goodreads, or Bookbub.

Other Wild Rose Press suspense-romances by Patricia McAlexander:

Stranger in the Storm (ebook only)
Shadows of Doubt

A word about the author…

Patricia McAlexander earned a bachelor's degree from The State University of New York at Albany, a master's from Columbia University, and a doctorate from The University of Wisconsin, Madison, all in English. After moving with her husband to Athens, Georgia, she taught composition and literature at The University of Georgia. Now retired, she has edited local newsletters and enjoys hiking, travel, and photography. But most of all she enjoys pursuing a childhood dream—writing novels.

https://patriciamcalexander.weebly.com

CPSIA information can be obtained
at www.ICGtesting.com
Printed in the USA
LVHW081603011122
732097LV00016B/768